THE
QUEEN OF
PUERTO RICO

THE
QUEEN OF
PUERTO RICO

And Other Stories

Joe Frank

WILLIAM MORROW AND COMPANY, INC.
NEW YORK

It is the policy of William Morrow and Company, Inc., and its imprints and affiliates, recognizing the importance of preserving what has been written, to print the books we publish on acid-free paper, and we exert our best efforts to that end.

Library of Congress Cataloging-in-Publication Data

Frank, Joe.
     The queen of Puerto Rico and other stories / Joe Frank.
          p.   cm.
     Contents: Tell me what to do — Fat man — Night — Date — Walter — The queen of Puerto Rico — The decline of Spengler — Philosophy.
     ISBN 0-688-08765-5
     I. Title.
PS3556.R33424Q4   1993
813′.54—dc20
                                                                          93-234
                                                                          CIP

Printed in the United States of America

First Edition

1 2 3 4 5 6 7 8 9 10

For my parents

Acknowledgments

My deepest gratitude goes to actor/director Arthur Miller, who has worked with me for years in radio and helped in creating and shaping much of the material for this book. "The Decline of Spengler," a collaborative radio play both written and improvised, would not have been possible without the contributions of Arthur and the rest of the cast, which included Lester Nafzger, Barbara Sohmers, David Rapkin, Charles Potter, Joseph Palmieri, Timothy Jerome, Leslie Cass, Avery Hart, Rosemary Foley, and Brother Theodore.

In the preparation of the material I was also fortunate to have the guidance, insights, and constructive editing of Larry Massett, Madeleine Lundberg, Tony Cohan, Larry Kusnitt, David Madole, Farley Ziegler, and Kathleen Morahan.

Special thanks also to Henry Dennis, Tom Strother, Kerry Breeze, Rusty Wayne, and Jack Cheeseborough for their contributions to the work.

I'm grateful to Ariana Morgenstern for her friendship and support.

Contents

CONTENTS

THE
QUEEN OF
PUERTO RICO

Tell Me What to Do

*A*fter work one Friday—she was frequently one of the last people to leave—she came into his office and sat down. She was wearing a raincoat, a pair of thick glasses, and a wide-brimmed hat that shaded her face. She slumped languorously in her chair. There was an odd twist to her mouth. He guessed she was in her mid-thirties, but she might have been older. When she removed her hat her hair was unkempt, and there was something slightly careless about her that he found both charming and annoying. She said she had recently come from Miami, where she had been the marketing director for a shopping center.

"And you came here because of a man," he said.

"You're absolutely right," she answered. "How did you know?"

She lit a cigarette and told him she had been involved with a South African stockbroker. When he moved to New York to work on Wall Street, they missed each other so much that she decided to leave her life in Miami and join him. But it hadn't worked. The relationship had soured. They argued endlessly. He was avoiding her, staying out late. Now she was about to move to a friend's apartment. To confuse things further, she had been offered a position at Citibank in Chicago, and the reason she was telling him all this was that she might need to take a few days off next week to fly to Chicago and check things out.

She told her story with wry amusement. She found it ironic that she had given up a terrific job in Miami to come to New York, and now she couldn't get along with her lover and had to move out. "If I accept the Citibank offer," she said, "I'll have to move again."

"Let's go for a drink," he said.

They walked to a bar. He was wearing his sunglasses. He wore them outdoors, indoors, day and night. He didn't like people to see his eyes, to know what he was feeling. She was wearing glasses too, with thick lenses that magnified her eyes. Once inside, she continued to wear her hat and raincoat.

She told him that last night she had picked up a huge black man at a downtown club. They had gone to his place but she couldn't remember much about it. "I know you're beginning to think of me in a certain way," she said, "but I'm not like that." When she arrived home at dawn, Gardner, her boyfriend, didn't ask where she'd been.

"But how did he feel about it?"

"He doesn't care."

"I don't believe it."

"No, he really wants me out."

Then she said she was afraid to go to Chicago. He asked her why, but she wouldn't explain.

At one point, he excused himself and walked to the phone booth on the corner to call his wife. When he returned, the door to the bar was locked. He looked at her through the window and she seemed like the kind of woman you see sitting by herself at the end of a bar when it closes down. He waved and the waiter let him in. He sat down beside her and told her he wanted to rent a room and make love to her. But she said she had to get up early the next morning to move her clothes into a friend's apartment. He asked for her number there. She wrote it down. Then he walked her out of the bar, hailed a taxi, and squeezed her hand. "Are you going home?" he asked. He wondered if she was going to another bar to pick up someone else.

"Yes, I'm going home," she said.

He watched her cab drive off and when he got back to his apartment that night and lay down next to his wife, all he could think of was her. He repeated her name, silently, over and over again, *Eve . . . Eve . . . Eve . . .*

He called her Saturday morning when Kathy was out. It was strange talking to her on the phone the first time. He asked if he could come over. She said, "Sure." Her apartment was on the third floor of a walk-up in the Village. She buzzed him in. When he came through the door she said, "We won't stay long." She was wearing slacks and a loose-fitting sweater. They both felt shy. He wondered, *What the hell am I doing here?* and sat down on the living-room couch.

She looked at him. "What's going on?"

"Let's not ask."

She poured him a Coke and asked if he wanted rum in it because that was her drink, Bacardi and Coke. He nodded. She turned on the radio, sat down next to him, and lit a cigarette. They listened to a jazz trio. When the piece was over he turned to her.

"How about sex?" he asked.

"What do you mean?"

"I mean you—me—here—now—doing it. Will we or won't we? If we're going to do it, let's do it now."

They were both still wearing their glasses.

"I'm a different kind of woman than you think I am," she said, and he wondered if she was confused about what kind of woman she really was. "Besides," she added, "there's not enough time."

"I can't leave here without holding and kissing you. What if we just make out?"

She looked down and smiled.

"No matter what happens," he said, "no matter what you want to do, we won't."

He took off his jacket, loosened his tie, and rolled up his sleeves.

"What are you doing? Getting ready for work?"

"Exactly," he said. He took off his sunglasses, she took off her thick glasses, and when he looked into her eyes and saw her face for the first time, she looked beautiful to him. She

16

moved into his arms, kissed him, and wrapped her legs around his thigh as if they had been making love for years.

They hugged and kissed for about ten minutes. Then he got up, rolled down his sleeves, put on his tie and jacket, and asked, "Are you still self-conscious?"

"No," she said.

They left the apartment. In the street, she got into a taxi and left.

At first he felt exhilarated. He thought of how beautiful she looked when she removed her glasses, and her kisses lingered with him. But as he walked home, he began to wonder about the ease with which she had wrapped herself around him. She had been too responsive. She had given herself over too easily. He couldn't help thinking she was an old pro, and the feeling lurked in him that maybe she did this with a lot of men.

At work on Monday, he waited impatiently for her to show up. When she arrived, she was distant and discreet. After all, he was her supervisor, a married man. He wrote her a card that said, "Tonight. A drink?" There were two boxes for her to check, "Yes" or "No." Later, he went to her desk to pick it up. She had checked the "Yes" box.

That evening they went to another bar. Now they were almost lovers. He wore his sunglasses and she wore her thick glasses, and as long as they kept their glasses on they were protected from each other. He asked about Gardner. She said he was forty, South African, divorced, and had two young daughters. She pointed at a man sitting at a table nearby, his head slumped forward on his chest. "That's like Gardner," she said. "He drinks all the time." Nevertheless, he earned

17

a considerable salary and was being groomed for an important position in his company. He paid the rent, purchased her clothes, and loaned her money.

"Has he been buying you?" he asked.

"No, but I think I'd make a good whore."

"Well, if you're looking for work, I have connections. Of course, I'd have to audition you first," he added. "What makes you think you'd make a good whore?"

"I know about men," she said, "and I think I'd enjoy it."

"It's a hard life," he said, "and it's lonely." The idea of her with different men was beginning to make him jealous.

Then she told him Gardner was leaving for Bangkok the next morning. He said it was on business, but she suspected it was for pleasure; shortly after moving into Gardner's apartment, she had found porno magazines, nude photos, and letters from women in a bureau drawer.

He shook his head, blew his breath out through pursed lips, and told her that Kathy was also leaving for Minneapolis Tuesday morning to attend a conference. They stared at each other. It was as if fate were whispering, *Here's an opening. Take it.*

"All right. I'm going to give you my address," he said, "and I want you to be there at eight o'clock tomorrow night."

She nodded and he had the impression she liked being told what to do.

In ten years of marriage he had never brought another woman to his apartment. If Kathy ever found out, she would be devastated. But somehow he didn't care. Besides, he told himself, he would be extremely careful, and what she didn't know couldn't hurt her. After Kathy left for the airport, he vacuumed, washed the dishes, changed the bedding, hid the wedding photos, and put all of her clothes in the back of the closet. He bought a quart of Bacardi and picked up a Chinese restaurant menu in case they wanted to order out. Then he wondered what would happen if one of his neighbors saw the cute blonde show up at his door.

Shortly after eight o'clock the doorman buzzed. He rang her through, put on some music, and turned down the lights. Candles flickered on the night table in the bedroom. He opened the door and she stood before him. Earlier, he had called Kathy in Minneapolis just to make sure she was really a thousand miles away.

He fixed drinks—Bacardi and Cokes—and sat on the sofa feeling tongue-tied. She sat across from him, lit a cigarette, and said, "So here we are." They stared at each other. Finally, he said, "Come over here." She gave him a little-girl pout and sat down next to him. He began stroking her hair, but she didn't respond. "Look, we're going to make love for the first time only once," he said, "so let's make it good. It'll never be like this again." He leaned forward, embraced her, and they began to kiss. Every so often she would back away from him as if to ask, "Who are you? What are we doing?"

She was so small and lithe that he picked her up easily and carried her into the bedroom, and from the moment he began making love to her he had the feeling she was a little girl of twelve. Her high, short shrieks were like a child's, and he wondered if the neighbors could hear. Then she began to ask him, "Tell me what you want . . . tell me what to do," and they made love all night long, until dawn.

*   *   *

In the morning, he decided they should leave the apartment separately. "This is what we'll do," he said. "You leave first, go downstairs, turn left, and walk south on Third Avenue. I'll leave five minutes later and catch up with you." He looked out the eyehole to make sure there was no one in the hall and then opened the door. She stood behind him in her raincoat, wide-brimmed hat, and thick glasses. "Okay," he said, and motioned for her to go. She passed him and he closed the door behind her. He waited about five minutes, walked down Third Avenue, and didn't see her anywhere. It was eight o'clock, the streets were empty, and he felt himself getting angry. *She walked the wrong way, damn it. She can't follow instructions. She's unreliable.* Then, with relief, he saw her at the corner. He jogged up the block, they hugged, and he felt strong, confident, as if he were expanding with love. It was a beautiful spring day. He told her how sweet she was and she rolled her eyes and said, "Please don't talk to me that way."

As she got in a cab, he said he was in love with her—words he never said to Kathy anymore, though he considered himself happily married and had no intention of leaving his wife. He closed the door and waved as she drove off.

Eating breakfast in a coffee shop, he started to rehash the night. He relived the first part of the evening when they had felt so uncomfortable, when they had stared at each other silently, and he thought, "I should have been more relaxed." Then he remembered their lovemaking. He had said, "Turn over. Get on your knees. Sit on the bureau. Open your mouth." And she had said, "Yes, sir. Right, sir. Okay, sir."

Once, she had curled up in his arms and asked him to just hold her, please hold her, and a fatherly feeling had come over him.

She had a pungent perfume—rich, sweet, and strong, one step away from being cheap. Normally he didn't like strong perfume, but he spent the rest of the morning hallucinating its scent. When he came home to pick up his briefcase for work, he smelled the living-room couch where she had sat, picked up the bedroom pillow, breathed in her odor, and felt energized, filled with strength.

He saw her at the office later that day. She was wearing a low-cut blouse and tight jeans. Suddenly the other men, who had never paid attention to her, were taking notice. He felt jealous. Was she going to make a pass at someone else? Work her way through the department? At the same time, he felt a sense of pride. She didn't need to protect herself with the hat and the raincoat anymore because she loved him and felt safe in his presence. They barely spoke to each other, but under the surface he knew they were both vibrating.

He was impressed by how good she was at dissembling, but also slightly saddened by it because it reminded him that she had probably done this before. He wanted to say, "Look, let's go back to my apartment, take off our clothes, get right back in bed, and take up where we left off." But he was afraid if he did, their affair might turn into something tawdry, and he didn't want to lose the magic. Last night he had said, "If this is the only night we spend together, it will be fine with me. You have your guy, and I have my gal." He had even suggested that it might be better as a romantic one-night adventure.

" 'We'll always have Paris,' " he'd said. But late in the afternoon he asked her to come back with him anyway.

It turned out she had friends she might have to see. He couldn't help wondering how it was possible, if she loved him the way he loved her, that seeing her friends could be as important as seeing him. *Did I imagine everything that happened last night?* "When will you know?" he asked. She wasn't sure. Her friends were supposed to call later that evening. If they called, she would have to see them. If they didn't, she would be free. He didn't believe her. *She's a creature of mood. She's not good at planning ahead. It all depends on how she's feeling at the moment.*

Ten minutes later, his phone rang. It was Leila, an old friend from college who wanted to go out for dinner. Leila was very attractive and he thought, *Okay, two can play this game.* So he told Leila to come over twenty minutes before the office closed.

When Leila arrived, he showed her around. He wanted to make Eve jealous, and he felt as if he were back in high school. Before they left, he went up to Eve's desk and said, "I'm going out to dinner. I'll be home by ten. If you want to meet, call me later." He gave her his unlisted home number and, for a moment, felt anxious. It occurred to him that late one night she'd call while he and Kathy were in bed.

Leila wanted to go back to his apartment rather than spend money in a restaurant. He found it interesting that when he entered his building with her he didn't worry about the doorman or the neighbors. He knew she was a friend and he didn't feel guilty about it. They had a few drinks and a salad and Leila was talking about her boyfriend when the phone rang.

He knew who it was and waited three rings before lifting the receiver.

She sounded a little drunk. *They didn't show up*, he thought, *and she went to a bar and has had a few.* She asked him about her Chicago job offer. What should she do? She had to decide tomorrow. "I can't discuss this with you now," he said. "Why don't you call back in an hour?" Then he hung up.

Leila stared at him. "Who was that?"

"A friend who's going through some changes at work."

Leila knew him well. She gave him a funny look.

About thirty minutes later, he heard the buzzer from downstairs. It felt like an electric shock. Leila turned to him. "More changes?"

He walked to the intercom. It was 10:00 P.M. He pressed the button and heard Eve's voice. "I'm here. Can I come up? I want to talk to you."

"No, I'll come down."

She laughed. "Why should you come down? I'll just come up."

"No," he said.

"Is someone there?"

"Yes. I'll buzz when it's time for you to come up."

He walked back into the living room. "I don't know how to say this, but someone's coming and you're going to have to go."

"It's all right," Leila said. "I understand."

She took her coat, kissed him on the cheek, and left.

He buzzed downstairs and a minute later Eve walked in.

"I didn't plan to come. Look what I wore. This old dress."

"Well, here you are," he said, thinking, *This woman is not to be trusted. She's unstable. She drinks too much. She shows up at my apartment uninvited. What will happen if something goes wrong and the relationship turns sour? What will she do? Will she arrive at work drunk and embarrass me?* He was flashing on horrible scenes of her storming into his office and demanding that he leave his wife. Or calling him late at night and hanging up whenever Kathy answered. Or mailing him angry postcards and threatening letters. Or waiting in the lobby of his building and, while he walked out with Kathy one day, rushing up and saying, "Look, we have to settle this right now." Kathy would look at him thinking, *What the hell is going on here?* and he would be trapped between the two of them with a lot of explaining to do. But he was secretly thrilled she had come over.

"Do you realize why I'm upset?"

"Because I came without calling."

At least she understood. They sat down and began discussing the job offer in Chicago. If she accepted, her relationship with Gardner was finished. The bank wanted her to start in two weeks. She had to let them know tomorrow. She was panic-stricken. Then she said there was another reason she didn't want to go to Chicago.

"Is there another man there?"

"Not exactly . . ." She faltered.

"Never mind. Let's forget about it. Let's put it behind us. Let's take the night and make the most of it."

They had a drink, went into the bedroom, and again, while they made love, she asked him repeatedly, "Tell me what you want. Tell me what to do."

*   *   *

They fell asleep at dawn. At eight o'clock he got up. The sun was coming through the blinds, yellow and soft and dream-like. She looked beautiful, like a sleeping child. He had to get to work early and he was not going to leave her alone in the apartment. He tried to rouse her gently but she didn't respond. He took a shower, got dressed, and tried to wake her again. It was eight-thirty. Finally, he shook her and said, "Come on. Get up."

She gave him a friendly but dirty look. "Let me sleep."

"I'm sorry, but we have to go."

She got dressed. He opened the door and checked the hall to make sure it was empty. She stood there half asleep in her raincoat, glasses, and hat. He gave her instructions.

"This time I want you to turn right, go to Lexington Avenue, walk downtown, and I'll pick you up in a taxi."

He closed the door behind her. Five minutes later, he went out. It was a chilly spring morning. He had that wasted, burned-out, no-sleep feeling. He hailed a cab, rode downtown, and didn't see her. *Oh, God, the stupid bitch. She turned the wrong way.* The cab drove around and around, but he couldn't find her.

At noon, he left work and walked to a restaurant two blocks from Gardner's apartment. He knew she had called in sick and was staying there while Gardner was in Bangkok. He dialed her number from a pay phone and heard Gardner's deep voice, in a heavy South African accent, on the answering machine. For a moment he was afraid to speak. Then he said, "I'm at the Coffee Bar. I missed you. Where were you?" He hung up and walked back to the office. Now she had two strikes against her—showing up at his house uninvited and either screwing up or deliberately not meeting him.

Around two in the afternoon, he was surprised to see her come in to work. They went through the same charade of acting like colleagues. When she walked by him at the end of the day he said, "Come into my office," and closed the door behind her.

"What happened?"

"This morning?"

"Yes, this morning."

She inhaled on her cigarette. "I was so annoyed at you for waking me up and telling me where to go, I decided to walk the other way." She laughed.

He liked her spirit and asked her out for a drink.

They went to a deserted bar around the corner. He sat with her by the window. There was a jukebox and a small dance floor. When a ballad came on, they rose from the table and began to dance. She was so light, so graceful. He felt as if they were imbued with light in the empty room.

"Do you know what I'd like to do?" she said. "I'd like to go out and have a real date tomorrow night, hit some bars and clubs, listen to music."

"Good. I'll take care of everything."

Friday morning she called in sick again. He wondered if she had decided to take the Chicago job after all. He phoned restaurants and jazz clubs and lined up the entire evening. But when he tried to reach her at home, there was no answer. He went back to his apartment and spent the night watching television.

Saturday morning, the day before Kathy and Gardner were due back, he phoned her again. She picked up.

After a long silence he asked, "What happened? Why didn't you call?"

"I tried you at work, but you were out for lunch. So I got busy with something else."

He felt angrier and angrier. "Remember when you told me you'd make a good whore? Well, I don't think you would because you're unreliable. Or were you too drunk to remember we made a date? Anyway, I'll see you sometime."

"Don't hang up," she said. "Can't we get through this?"

"Probably," he answered, "but I don't feel like getting through it now." He slammed down the receiver and stood in his kitchen feeling awful. He had to respect her ambivalence. Unless he wanted to ruin what had happened between them or make it look cheap, he had to call her back. He dialed her number again.

"Listen," he said. "Do you want to have breakfast at Lemons?"

"All right. But give me fifteen minutes to get dressed."

He took a cab to Lemons and asked for a table in the back. When she showed up, they split an order of eggs Benedict. She had a club soda. He had a Bloody Mary. Then he took off his sunglasses and looked at her, and she took off her thick glasses and looked at him. "Let's go back to my place," he said. "I want to make love to you right now. Will you come with me?"

She nodded. "But first I have to go back to my house. I left clothes in the dryer."

"I'll go with you." He had the feeling that if he didn't stay with her, he would never see her again.

He didn't feel comfortable going into Gardner's apartment and decided to wait downstairs in the lobby. He would give her five minutes.

When the five minutes were up, he hailed a taxi. He sat in the back for what seemed an eternity, convinced she would never come downstairs and that she was doing another number on him. He began muttering, "Women, those bitches. Damn it."

Finally, she came out, got in the cab, and they drove to his apartment. They walked into the lobby past the doorman and rode up the elevator. In the corridor, he heard his neighbor's door being unlocked and realized someone was about to come out. He rushed into his apartment and closed the door in Eve's face, leaving her alone in the hall. He assumed she would know what to do.

He heard Eve and his neighbor, Virginia, exchange pleasantries and get on the elevator together. Then it occurred to him that Eve might not come back. He looked out the window and paced absently in the living room until the doorbell rang. He unlocked the door and she stood there, giggling. It was two in the afternoon. They sat in the living room smoking cigarettes. She had a drink. Then she began to talk about her relationship with Gardner and whether or not she should go to Chicago. Again she said there was a reason she didn't think she could go.

"What is it?"

They sat in silence listening to music on the radio. Then she sighed and told him she had been molested by her father. It happened while she was growing up in Chicago. He had begun to fondle her when she was two or three, and had continued until she was eleven. Nobody in the family knew. At least three times a week he would come into her bedroom at night. *This is what fathers and daughters do*, she thought.

He had the feeling her story was hard to tell, but that it was not the first time she had told it. As she spoke he flashed on their nights together, and how much she was like a little girl trying to please him. He found it exciting and wanted to make love to her again.

Finally she had told her mother. The two of them moved to Miami. She never saw her father again. And the reason she didn't want to return to Chicago was that she knew her father was still there and she was afraid of what might happen if they met. She was terrified she might start with him again and never be able to stop.

They undressed and got into bed, and as they made love he encouraged the father-daughter feeling by the way he held her, cuddled with her, and told her what to do. He knew her father had given her lots of instructions, too.

On Sunday he went to pick up Kathy at the airport. He was relieved to see her. She looked wonderful. They drove back to the apartment. He had changed the sheets and pillowcases and had washed his clothes, but he could still smell Eve's perfume and wondered if Kathy could smell it, too. That night they made love more passionately than they had for years. During the next month their love life improved. "I should go away more often," she said.

He saw Eve at work on Monday. That night they went to another bar. They were both wearing their glasses and smoking cigarettes. Gardner was back in town and wanted to see her, and soon he would have to go back to Kathy. He felt that tragic "it's over" feeling. *We had our fling, and now it's ended.* They talked about running away and the beautiful places they could visit. "We'll take your credit card. I'll clean out my bank account. And then," he said, "we'll go right to the airport."

She took off her glasses and he took off his sunglasses and they looked at each other eye-to-eye. The jukebox played something slow. "Do you want to dance?" he asked. She nodded. They stood up in the middle of the room and held each other tightly, and he felt exhilaration, sadness, and loss. He looked at her. "Do you realize we had a whole love affair in one week? We met, we made love, we fought, we parted, we made up, and now it's over and we did the whole thing in six days."

They left the bar. He hailed a taxi and shook her hand. As she stepped into the cab, he caught the scent of her perfume. Before she drove off, she said she and Gardner were going to Miami. She was still trying to stall the Citibank people in Chicago. Ever since Gardner had come back, he had been nicer to her.

"Be sure and let me know what happens," he said.

He didn't hear from her for a week and found himself writing her name over and over again on scraps of paper. He took out the folder that contained her original application and studied her résumé and the forms she had filled out in her little-girl's handwriting, simple and shaky. He thought of how, when he had first seen her, she meant nothing to him. Now he was in love with her and couldn't stop smelling her perfume and dreaming about her eyes and her body and her hands. But he tried to put her behind him.

A week later, she called the office. He closed the door, lifted the phone, and heard her husky cigarette voice. "Gardner asked me to marry him."

"I knew it."

"How?"

"The same way I knew the reason you came to New York, the same way I've known everything about you."

A few days later, she came by to clean out her desk. He led her into his office. They sat down and she told him about the night Gardner proposed. They had gone out to celebrate, and he had gotten drunker than she had ever seen him before. When they got back to the apartment it took two doormen to lift him out of the cab and carry him upstairs. Her voice broke and tears filled her eyes. She was terrified.

"Gardner is like your father."

She nodded.

They took off their glasses, looked at each other, and were both on the verge of crying when he said, "Get out of here. Come on. Hurry up. Leave this office. Don't say anything. Don't kiss me. Just go, fast." He said it, smiling, the way you might say, *Get out of here, you maniac, you knucklehead.*

She stood up. He held her in an awkward embrace. Then she was gone.

He spoke to her one more time the following week when she called to tell him Gardner wanted her to take the job at Citibank after all. They were going to move to Chicago together.

*　　*　　*

One evening when he returned from a business trip, he found the apartment stripped. All the furniture was gone except for the bed, the TV, and the dinette set. On the counter he saw a hand-written note from Kathy. She wrote that during the last few years she had grown increasingly lonely. Three months ago during the conference in Minneapolis, she had met a wonderful man. She had never felt like this before with anyone and could never forgive herself if she didn't take this chance at happiness. "You really can't blame me," she added. "After all, you won't have to sneak around telling me any more lies. Hope you had as much fun as I had in Minneapolis."

He spent the next few weeks feeling numb. He went to work and came home to the bare cell of his apartment. Kathy refused to speak to him except through her lawyer.

It was Monday evening. He was about to leave work when his phone buzzed. The receptionist said, "It's a Mrs. McLean." In their last conversation before Eve left for Chicago, he had told her, "Okay, from now on, you're Mrs. McLean." He waited a moment, then lifted the receiver. His heart was racing. He realized he had been waiting for this call for months.

"Do you know who this is?" she asked.

He wondered if he should pretend he didn't and force her to tell him.

"Of course I do."

"Are you happy I called?"

"I'm delighted."

He said it in a flat tone because he didn't want her to know whether he was being polite or sincere. He couldn't bear to reveal how much he was moved by the sound of her voice.

"I'll be in New York for a convention the day after tomorrow," she said. "Would you like to get together?"

He suggested breakfast or lunch rather than ask about meeting at night. She said she would be flying in at 7:00 P.M. Wednesday evening, would be in meetings all day Thursday, and was scheduled to go on to Miami Thursday night. "I tried you at the office earlier in the week," she added, "but I couldn't get through." It occurred to him that she was a habitual liar. He remembered how she always waited a beat before answering his questions, as if she were trying to come up with a plausible answer. But he also knew those pauses were often caused by her smoking. They decided she would call him when she got in on Wednesday night. She said she was looking forward to seeing him, but neither spoke of what might happen when they met.

Her call had come just as he was getting used to Kathy's absence. He had even begun to think about Eve again, to remember the week they spent together, running and rerunning it through his mind, trying to correct the mistakes he had made and changing what had happened to suit more appealing fantasies. He should have been rougher, tied her up, taken his time, teased her more. Again he was haunted by doubts and second thoughts and the vague suspicion that she had used him to make Gardner jealous. But the idea of making love to her all night and doing all the things he imagined in his daydreams overwhelmed him. He knew she wasn't good for him. Meeting her again would just deepen his frustration, and he took perverse satisfaction in knowing it would probably end badly.

He also tried to reconcile himself to the possibility of their just talking in the hotel bar, because he didn't want to spend their time together thinking about whether he would be able to make love to her. Going through the motions of trying to get laid would be too degrading. And he was afraid that was exactly what would happen. He tried to reassure himself. "Maybe we'll make love. Maybe we won't. It doesn't matter. That's not really important." But the words rang hollow.

Wednesday night, around eight, his phone rang.

"I'm at the hotel," she said. She sounded tense.

"Don't be scared. Everything's going to be okay. Did you just come in?"

"Yes, I took a cab from the airport."

"Get yourself together. Unpack. Relax. Call me when you're ready."

"Where do you want to meet?"

"At the hotel," he said. "In the lobby."

As soon as they hung up he was sure she would call back and cancel, so he decided to catch a cab and phone her from the hotel lobby. *Don't go there thinking about going to bed,* he told himself on the ride downtown.

When he arrived he thought of taking the elevator to her floor, knocking on her door, and walking right in. It would give him an advantage. But he decided to call her from downstairs instead.

"Hi. I'm in the lobby. I'll wait for you in the bar."
She didn't seem surprised. *She knew I'd come*, he thought.

He walked into the dimly lit bar. The room was crowded.
A female bartender in a bow tie and a vest served drinks. The
pianist, wearing a tuxedo, his face pale, and his features finely
chiseled, looked like an aging chorus boy. People sat on stools
around the baby grand singing show tunes.

He sat down at an empty table in the corner and waited for
Eve. As the minutes passed, he grew more and more nervous.
He felt lonely, stupid, and naked. "Why am I here?" he
wondered. "What good can come of it?" At the same time,
the moment seemed full of promise. He looked around the
room and wondered if there were other people there who felt
the way he did. An attractive woman sat alone at a nearby
table and he thought of going to the hotel phone, calling Eve,
and saying, "I'm leaving, don't come down," then rushing
back to ask the woman if she would care to join him.

He decided to plan the evening around Eve's drinking.
During her first two drinks, he would keep the conversation
light. By the third drink, he would suggest going back to her
room. Then it would take two more drinks to get her into
bed. He thought of it as a long-distance race in which he
would have to pace himself and realized he was using her just
as he had been afraid she had been using him. Again he asked
himself, *Why am I here? What do I want? Is this just about getting laid?* Maybe the reason he wanted to go to bed with her
was to break through the nonsense, to find her through physical intimacy. They were both troubled, lonely, insecure. They

were also spoiled children who wanted to see how naughty and fucked up they could be. But there was something poignant, he thought, about two people caught in a cycle of self-destruction. It sounded tragic and romantic.

Finally, she came into the bar. She was wearing a white blouse, a paisley scarf, a gray business skirt, and a blue blazer. Her hair was pulled back and she had put on her glasses. He had brought his sunglasses with him, too, but it was so dark in the bar he had decided not to wear them. She looked tired. He tried to pull a chair up for her. "Relax," she said. "It's all right." Her tone was patronizing. It made him feel that she had already seized the advantage.

He asked how she was doing. She said she was miserable. She hated her job, the marriage wasn't working, they had no friends, and all they did was drink and fight and make love. She was ready to end it. "I'm not in love with him," she said. Every morning, she had to get up and fix breakfast, drive Gardner to his office, then drive to her own job on the other side of town. At work, she had almost nothing to do. "I've been given enough rope to hang myself," she said. In the evening she would meet Gardner in a bar and they would drink, go to dinner, come home, and continue to drink until Gardner passed out or they had a fight or made love. Later, she would be unable to sleep. Then it would be morning and the same thing would begin again. And why did he need all that pornography? She tried to please him in every way. They made love *all the time*. What was wrong with him?

She was drawn to him because of the money, the apartment, the clothes, the restaurants, the car, and the opportunity to travel. But she was going to draw the line. On Thursday Gardner was supposed to meet her in Miami. If he didn't show up she would get a divorce.

She had already had an affair in San Francisco two months ago. A man picked her up in the hotel bar and they spent the night in her room. She told him she didn't want to get involved with anyone because she was having problems with her husband, and they both laughed at the irony of it, the paradox of not wanting to have an affair because your marriage was in trouble. When she came back to Chicago the man began to call her, but she didn't want to have anything to do with him. She thought Gardner suspected something, but she was sure he had been unfaithful, too. They were both pretending they didn't care about the other's infidelities, but it wasn't working.

Then she told him about her visit to a psychiatrist. The doctor said she had a drinking problem. "But what do you think?" he had asked.

"I don't think that's true," she had said. "I think the problem is Gardner. If I can solve things with Gardner, I can take care of the drinking."

As he listened to her story, he had a strong feeling the reverse was true. But he didn't want to talk about it because if they discussed her drinking he would never get her into bed. He hated the fact that he was trying to take advantage of her for his own purposes.

She was caught in a trap, she said, and didn't know whether or not she had made it for herself. She had pursued Gardner for so long that when he finally proposed, she had to accept. She had gotten everything she wanted—and she was miserable. It was funny, she said, and he admired her for being able to laugh at herself. He watched her continue to talk, her words seeming to blur together, and thought of how much she looked like both an innocent child and a worldly-wise, over-drunk, and overfucked woman.

Then she asked how he was doing. He was supposed to tell her about his job and his wife, but he knew she didn't really care. It was just intermission. Their conversations always centered on her. The first time they met they had discussed her relationship with Gardner, where she was going to stay after she left him, and how she was in crisis but was bearing up beautifully. Now the same thing was happening again. He wondered if her whole life was like this.

He ran down his own feeble story—leaving out Kathy's desertion. Then she leaned forward, looked soulfully into his eyes, and asked him to sit next to her. *She's controlling the whole thing,* he thought. He got up, sat down beside her, and she held his hand in both of hers like a dear friend.

She was on her fourth drink, one drink past the plan, and they were nowhere near going to her room. He had a sinking feeling as he listened to her repeat the same themes: Gardner and she were lonely. They drank, they fought, they fucked. She realized how self-destructive it was and wanted to get away but didn't know how. Then she added there was another reason she felt sick about being in Chicago and repeated the story of how her father had molested her, and he felt as if a cloud were descending over him.

"What exactly did he do?" he asked.

She told him he had penetrated her with his fingers and had forced her to masturbate him. He asked if she had enjoyed it. She said she hadn't really understood what was going on and thought it was something fathers and daughters did. "I didn't know it was so weird," she said.

"Did you ever have an orgasm?"

"Yes."

"How old were you?"

"Around ten."

Three hours had passed. She was on her fifth drink. He wondered if, years later, she would tell him the story a third time. Then he decided it was time to act. He asked for the check. She offered to pay.

"No," he said.

She seemed reluctant to go back to her room, but he managed to shepherd her into the elevator, down the corridor, and through her door. No sooner had he closed it behind them than he walked to the phone and ordered four more drinks. Then he opened the window and looked down over filthy rooftops and a thin stream of traffic heading up Sixth Avenue. The air was heavy with humidity and he heard distant thunder.

She asked about Kathy. For a moment he wondered whether to tell her what had happened, then described how he had returned home to find Kathy's note and the stripped apartment. Right away he knew he had made a mistake. Now that Kathy had abandoned him, he looked weak. If Kathy didn't want him anymore, why should Eve? He could sense something in her eyes, as if she were seeing him in a new light. It made him want to hurt her.

The drinks arrived. This time he let her pay because he was losing patience. When the waiter left, he walked over to where she was lounging in a chair by the bed, took her in his arms, and began to kiss her. She yielded, melting into his arms, then pulled away. "Look," she said. "I don't think we can do this tonight. I'm having my period."

"I don't give a damn about your period," he said. "Don't give me that period crap. That's the stupidest excuse I've ever heard."

He grabbed her again, kissed her, and carried her to the bed. He lay down on top of her and put his knee between her legs. She didn't move. He pulled back, gazed into her eyes, and kissed her face. She looked tired and scared. "Please stop," she whispered.

"You'd sooner fuck a stranger than fuck me," he said. Then he remembered the cab ride and how he had tried to prepare himself for this possibility. He asked her to hold him, just hold him, and she put her arms around him and stroked him gently. Then he realized he was soaked with sweat and went into the bathroom to wash off.

When he came out, she was asleep—or making believe she was asleep—fully clothed under the covers. He knew she had to get up at eight o'clock in the morning and it was well past three. He kissed her on the forehead, whispered, "Goodbye," and left the room. He rode down the elevator feeling small, feeble, cynical, and angry. He seemed to be drowning in the odor of her perfume and tried to brush it off his clothes and wave it away from him. Then he walked down the lobby and through the revolving door. Outside, a storm had broken. A few people were huddled under the canopy. The doorman was standing in the street holding an umbrella, trying to flag down cabs.

There was a subway stop a few blocks away and he decided

to run for it. He took a deep breath and plunged into the street. Three blocks away, gasping, he stopped under the marquee of an X-rated movie house. His clothes were drenched. He watched the rain slanting in the wind. Traffic moved slowly along the avenue and he heard the distant siren of an ambulance. He thought: *I do not want to go home* and ducked into the theater.

Fat Man

*A*aron tries to sleep as long as possible. When he feels himself rousing, the sunlight flush against the closed blinds, he wraps his pillow around his ears and lifts the blanket over his head, leaving a small opening for his mouth and nose, like a cowl. He doesn't want to wake up because the hours between eight and ten are the hardest to get through, the streets below crowded with people going off to work while he has nothing to do, nothing to look forward to. So if he can get through them by sleeping, he can curb the panic he feels every morning. He won't go to the bathroom because he knows if he does he may never get back to sleep, and when he finally does wake up, it's with a sense of sadness that he has to face another day.

Then comes the period of lying in bed holding the remote

control watching television. He flicks from one station to another, past game shows, cartoons, reruns of popular old programs, and local interviews. While he watches, he forgets himself—it's almost like sleeping again—and he imagines millions of the unemployed and the aged looking at television to stop thinking. But for him it doesn't hold. His mind is too active. So he gets up and begins pacing from one end of his apartment to the other. By now it might be eleven-thirty in the morning and, to pass the time, he'll go into the kitchen and cook himself an omelet with bacon, fried potatoes, corn muffins, orange juice, and fresh coffee. He may not even be hungry, but he wants to give himself something to do, to keep busy, to fill at least another thirty or forty minutes. Or sometimes he'll walk to a luncheonette near his apartment wearing his dark sunglasses, ratty overcoat, running shoes, and baseball cap. He'll buy a paper at the counter, order a meal, and sit as far away from other people as possible, reading and eating.

When Aaron was younger, he looked at other people going about their business and thought, *You poor slobs. You're rushing to do something, to get somewhere, and where are you going? You're hurrying to work where you'll have to kiss someone's ass and someone else will stab you in the back. You're racing to make enough money so you can rush out and spend it. And I don't have to worry about any of that. I'm a free spirit. I can observe the human comedy on the street and just float through it as if it's my own little movie.*

But over the years, his attitude changed. He began to feel lonely and envious because everyone else seemed to be moving in some direction, making an effort, and now he sees them in the mornings dressed in business suits, carrying briefcases, filing into subway stations and looking for taxis, and he feels like a person from another planet.

He went to a small college in Iowa. It was in the sixties. He didn't take part in the marches and sit-ins, but still saw himself as a rebel.

In his freshman year, he drove back to Manhattan on Thanksgiving. It was a long trip, more than fourteen hours. The car was packed with students. Their first stop was a service area just outside Cleveland. They sat at the counter of a Howard Johnson's restaurant looking at a sign that listed more than fifty kinds of ice cream. Aaron, to the amusement of his friends, asked for even more exotic flavors. "Could I please have a broccoli-mint-apple-pie-cobbler? No, wait. I think I'd prefer the orange-sunburst-chicken-nut-fudge crunch. Or perhaps the pistachio-fried-egg-okra delight with dehydrated applesauce topping and stewed lungs?"

It started as an accident. There was a stack of brownies on the counter wrapped in cellophane. Aaron took one and meant to pay for it, but realized on his way back to the car that he had forgotten. Rather than go back, he unfolded the cellophane and ate it. At the next service area, he stole two more brownies to share with his friends. At the third stop, he borrowed a purse from one of the girls, held it in his lap at the counter, filled it with a dozen brownies from the display platter, and passed it back to her. Finally, just outside New York, he emptied an entire platter of brownies into his bookbag. The restaurants were so busy that no one noticed. As they drove, he and his classmates munched on the chocolate. But they could only eat so many and he soon found himself with a surplus.

By the time he got back to college, Aaron had accumulated so many brownies he thought he'd build something out of them. But he didn't know what. All he knew was that he needed more. So whenever he drove home for vacations, he stopped at every Howard Johnson's coming and going to steal as many brownies as he could, and over a period of a year he amassed two steamer trunks full. The brownies got hard and stale, but they didn't rot. He banded them together, the way they stack money in bank-heist movies. Eventually, his brownie collection became famous. Students from all over the campus came to look at it. His only problem was that, by next fall, the brownies began to stink up his room. The odor of stale chocolate was in his clothes, his shoes, his hair. He couldn't stand the smell and decided to get rid of them. But he didn't want to just throw them out. He wanted to do something whimsical and original, to feed his reputation as a campus legend. Finally, he came up with an idea: He'd return them.

That Thanksgiving vacation he placed one of the trunks in his car and set out on the journey home with a new sense of mission. Now every time he stopped at a Howard Johnson's, he would fill the pockets of his shirt, overcoat, and pants with brownies, walk in, sit down at the counter, and, while he sipped a Coke, furtively empty his pockets, adding his own stale brownies to those displayed on the platters in front of him. Soon all the students knew of his project. He was the talk of the college. They thought it was a great idea, and they were all behind him.

Both Thanksgiving and Christmas went well. He managed to return one and a half trunks of brownies because he and his friends stopped at every service area in both directions between Cedar Rapids and New York. Then, during Easter, he arrived at the first Iowa Howard Johnson's rest stop, his pockets filled with the dry chocolate squares, but the brownie platters were gone. He was stunned. Were they on to him? He looked around, half expecting to be seized by security, when he noted with relief that the brownies had been moved to the candy counter in front of the cash register. It was too risky to add his stolen brownies to the stacks in front of the cashier, so he sat down at the counter and ordered dinner. When he finished his meal, he polished his plate with his napkin and, holding the plate in his lap, stacked his brownies—Howard Johnson's–style—on it, put it back on the counter, paid the check, and left.

At the next plaza, his friends helped him. They argued heatedly with the cashier, claiming they'd been overcharged, while Aaron reached into the deep pockets of his overcoat, drew out dozens of stale brownies, and placed them on the shelves over the lollipops, Caramello bars, and maple sugar people. By the summer, he managed to return every brownie he'd stolen.

And it wasn't long before Howard Johnson's restaurants were converted into cafeterias with pay toilets and cheap air driers in the bathrooms, and not long after that he saw them closing down. Although he realized it was because of the expanding fast-food industry—the McDonald's, Burger Kings, Pizza Huts, Taco Bells, Kentucky Fried Chicken outlets, and all the rest—he felt a bittersweet sense of victory.

He knew he had played his small part in the decline of a great American institution.

A movie comes on at one in the afternoon and he turns on the TV to see what it is. He won't look in the paper in advance because he doesn't want to know ahead of time that it might be a film he won't like. He wants to hold out hope for as long as possible that he'll be able to fill the hours between one and three, and sometimes he watches television all afternoon, lying in bed with the blinds closed until the sun goes down behind the buildings.

If a friend is planning to drop by, he takes out his guitar and amp, plugs them in, and covers his desk with scribbled yellow pads and a phone book so it looks as if he's been writing songs and making calls. But if no one's expected and he doesn't want to watch the one o'clock movie, he goes out for a walk, unwashed and unshaven, envying the Skid Row bums he passes because they have nothing to worry about anymore, having left their careers and futures far behind. He thinks it might be a relief to be a tramp wrapped in a blanket, lying in the warmth of a subway grating, listening to the sound of a passing train.

In the evening he likes to get stoned because his sense of time disappears. He no longer worries about how he'll make it through the next few hours, or that life is passing him by and he's blowing it with each minute he lives, or that more and more people are younger than he is—doctors, lawyers, journalists, artists, professors, businessmen. He can just sit in his living room feeling a mild, euphoric buzz. He doesn't mind the mess. He doesn't worry about putting things away. He plays his guitar or listens to music and recalls amusing things from the past.

After he left college in Iowa, Aaron came back to Manhattan. It was fall. He moved into a small walk-up apartment in the Village and enrolled in a few courses at Columbia. His mother paid his tuition and helped out with expenses. But he needed a job. One afternoon, he checked the student bulletin board and saw a listing for a part-time janitor and gardener at the Cathedral of St. John the Divine. The church, its rectory, school, and outbuildings were spread over six acres of land near the campus. He applied for the position and was hired.

Each day he would leave his apartment at 5:00 A.M. wearing his madras jacket, chinos, and white bucks. Carrying a briefcase, he would ride the subway to 110th Street and walk from Broadway to the church. The city was dark, the streetlamps still lit. The wind whipped the trees. He liked being out early in the morning. After changing into his work clothes, his first job was to clean the rectory. He mopped the hallways, vacuumed the offices, and emptied the wastebaskets. There were radios in most of the rooms, and he tuned them all to his favorite pop station, working his way through the building to the sounds of rock 'n' roll.

He usually got to the kitchenette around 6:30 A.M., just as he was growing hungry. While he cleaned up, he'd help himself to a few cookies, a cupcake, or a doughnut from the refrigerator. After a few weeks, his boss, Mr. Wilkes, asked to speak with him because people had complained that food was missing. He denied taking anything and stopped doing it, but not right away, so suspicion wouldn't fall on him.

When he finished his janitorial tasks, around 7:00 A.M., he took his rake and sack, walked out onto the grounds, and while the sun rose and the city came to life, he raked leaves, stuffed them into his bag, and burned them in the incinerator.

After work, Aaron changed back into his student outfit and went to a campus hangout called the Brass Rail. He took a table in the corner, ate breakfast, and studied until his first class. It was there he met Greta, a tall, blond German waitress. She often looked pale and wasted after a night of partying. She smoked Camels, wore no makeup, picked her teeth with a toothpick, and drank a lot of coffee. Her hands shook slightly. She told him she'd been on her own for years, ever since her father, a left-wing intellectual, had lost his teaching position in Hamburg. She liked to drink Black Russians, listen to classical music, and talk about the men she dated and the places they made love. She also spoke of becoming an artist, but he never saw her paint anything and she never showed him any of her work.

Early one morning, having spent the night in her room near the campus, he said, "Come with me. I'll show you what I do." They walked to the church. It was late fall, cold, and still dark out. He led her into the rectory and she helped him clean up. He felt very decadent and romantic—a Jewish student gardener working alongside a crazy German woman in a church built in honor of a Christian saint while rock music echoed from radios throughout the building. She helped him mop the hallways and they scrubbed the laundry room and cleaned the office of the newsletter. When he started vacuuming the library, she stood behind him gently caressing the back of his neck with her fingers. Then she took off her sweater, unfastened the top buttons of her blouse, and kissed him.

He made some coffee in the kitchenette, walked back to the library, and she sat down on his lap and began to fondle him. He kissed her, slipped her blouse from her shoulders, and removed her tights and shoes. She lay down on a large oak table in the study, and whispered to him in German. He unbuckled his belt and unzipped his fly, his pants dropping in a heap at his feet. He looked down at her, savoring the sight of her body, when the door at the other end of the room opened and an old man in a flowing black robe appeared. Greta continued to moan in German. The priest took one long steady look, turned away, his gown making a swishing sound, and was gone.

A week later, Mr. Wilkes fired him for stealing food. He said, "We checked with the night watchman and we know there's no other way the food could have disappeared. I'm afraid you're through." No mention was made of Greta in the library. So he lost his job. Then Greta left town. He never found out where she went and never heard from her again.

Sometimes when Aaron's out walking, he wanders into a drugstore and browses through magazines, looks at clocks, cassette players, and radios locked behind plate glass, and tries on different pairs of sunglasses. The sunglasses he now wears he stole from the drugstore on the corner. He put them on one day, looked at himself in the mirror, liked them, and continued to wander around the store wearing them, the price tag dangling down over his nose, until he finally walked out.

Once, he tried on a pair of jeans in a dressing room, tore

off the plastic tag that sets off the alarm, put his own jeans on over them, walked to the front to pick up the bags he'd checked, flirted with a salesgirl, and left. Sometimes he goes to a large, busy luncheonette, orders scrambled eggs, pancakes, bacon, sausages, home-fried potatoes, toast, and coffee, eats his meal, gets a bill for it, moves to another seat at the counter and orders coffee and a Danish. Then, at the cashier, he pays the amount on the second check.

One afternoon, he found a purse in the gutter with fifty dollars and credit cards, and he pocketed the money, and sold the cards to a friend. It happened when he was playing the ukulele in a department store. He wore a T-shirt with the store's logo on it and sang the store's theme song. He was posted next to the gift shop and managed, over a period of a few weeks, to steal brass paperweights, leather-bound address books, calendars, pens, and boxes of stationery.

Then, for a while, he had a job raising money for a symphony orchestra. He sat at one of about twenty tables with beige telephones in a fluorescent-lit room and called season ticket holders, subscribers to the monthly magazine, members of the Conductors' Club, and people who had bought a gift from the orchestra catalog.

Once he dialed a number and heard a message on tape. "This is a recording. Due to a recent operation, Miss Higgins is unable to speak. However, she can hear you. So please leave a message." Then he heard a *click* as someone picked up the phone. Normally, he was supposed to hang up on answering machines, but he hadn't made a sale for an hour, and he was getting nervous. "Hello, Miss Higgins?" he said. "If you can hear me, please tap once."

And he heard, *Click*.

"Miss Higgins, I'm calling from the symphony in New York City. Did you receive the letter from our president, Mr. Bronstein? Please tap once for yes and twice for no."

Click.

"Good. Do you approve of the aims of the program?"

Click.

"Wonderful. Mr. Bronstein, in his letter, spoke of the many ways in which people can become involved in the symphony. One, for example, is a pledge of two percent of your annual income once a year for the next three years. How do you feel about this guideline?"

Click.

"I'm glad you approve. Would that be a pledge you'd feel comfortable making?"

Click, click.

"Then let's find something more appropriate. Is that all right?"

Click.

"How would you feel about a pledge of one thousand dollars once a year?"

Click, click.

"How about three hundred and fifty dollars twice a year?"

Click, click.

"How about a pledge of four hundred dollars annually, two hundred twice a year? A lot of people are doing it that way."

Click, click.

She finally accepted the lowest possible contribution of $50 per year.

"I'll send you a formal statement of your pledge tomorrow,"

he said, "and thank you for your very generous gift. Have a pleasant evening."

Click.

Many of the people he called were old, ailing music lovers who would tell him about their accidents, illnesses, and hospitalizations. Some, in the middle of a conversation, would break into horrible fits of coughing. When they recovered they would say that, as much as they wanted to, they couldn't afford to help the symphony. Besides, they didn't expect to live another three years.

He worked from 8:00 to 11:00 P.M. at $4.50 an hour, sitting in a group of middle-aged women, college students, unemployed actors, failed pianists, and people who claimed they were businessmen, professors, and lawyers who, for one reason or another, were between engagements. There were also a few street people. One of them, a black man whose eyes would sometimes roll up into his head in the middle of a phone call, sat at a desk pointing his forefinger and squinting as if he were aiming a pistol. Then he would depress his thumb, shooting down his co-workers one by one.

When you go into a subway station, you enter a hole in the ground. It's damp. Every sound echoes. You feel as if you're in an altered state of consciousness. Time seems to stand still, yet your sense of it is heightened. You look around and see that people's behavior is similar to that of animals in cages. Some pace absently up and down while others sit on benches or lean against a wall or a pillar, staring blankly into space. The platform is dimly lit. There are tile walls, concrete floors, and an endless succession of columns and girders, lines of force stretching in front of you and down into the tunnel. You can see that the subway stations were originally fine examples of innovative architecture. Now they're filthy and defiled. In the old days, the cars had fans, stuffed wicker seats, and handles on leather straps. That, too, has changed. Now the seats are cast from plastic and the handles are of metal. And the pelvic movement necessary to push your way through a turnstile has a peculiarly suggestive feel. After all, if one were to remove the turnstile but make everyone go through the same motion as they passed into the subway, the sight of strangers queuing up to take a strong pelvic thrust at one another from behind would serve as an apt metaphor for the human condition.

Early morning in the subway is a special time. The stations seem cleaner, the air fresher. From 4:30 to 6:30 A.M. are the hours when the night and day people cross paths, when the tired partygoers, musicians, waitresses, janitors, night watchmen, pimps, and whores meet the early morning shift of workers, domestics, and students who have to travel a long way. Aaron liked standing on the platform and riding the trains at that time, and that's what he misses most when he thinks about his job at the church.

He likes the idea of an underground city, the sense of living in an artificial environment that might have been built after a nuclear holocaust, with long stretches of hallways, multilevel ramps, railings, and escalators. In some of the larger stations, they sell food, clothes, books, records, newspapers, magazines, and candy. You can buy a token, go into the subway, and travel anywhere under the city for years, as long as you never come out.

*   *   *

Three years ago, Aaron's mother disconnected her phone and swallowed over one hundred Tuinals. When her friend Dora called, the phone just rang and rang. After trying for three hours, Dora walked to her apartment a few blocks away and buzzed the door. She had keys to both locks. After waiting a minute, she took a deep breath and let herself in. She found Aaron's mother barely conscious, lying on the bed. Spread out beside her were bankbooks, financial statements, and a will. "Let me die," she moaned. "I want to die."

"Well, if you're going to go, dear, you better go quickly," Dora said, "because I'm calling 911."

Ten minutes later, an ambulance arrived and his mother, now unconscious, was taken to the hospital. Aaron was asleep when Dora called. "Your mother is in New York Hospital," she said. "It's an emergency."

Aaron took a cab uptown. A young intern met him at the door of the intensive care unit. He told Aaron that by the time they'd pumped his mother's stomach, she'd already digested most of the medication. At this point, it was a matter of waiting. "She'll probably be out for at least eight to ten hours," he said, "so you might as well go home. There's nothing anybody can do." Aaron suspected the doctor had contempt for suicides. He could see it in his eyes, hear it in his voice. He also felt implicated, as if the doctor thought that he, in some way, might be responsible.

"I'd like to see her," Aaron said.

They walked down a corridor to a room where she lay on a bed in a curtained-off area. She had a tube down her throat attached to a ventilator that was breathing for her. Her throat looked swollen, and her head was bent as if her neck had been broken. Electrodes were fastened to her chest and he could see the lit pattern of her heartbeat as it moved across a nearby screen. There was an IV in her arm hooked to a bag on a pole. A tube from a catheter drained urine from her bladder. She was wearing a hospital gown and looked oddly small, as if she'd shrunk.

Aaron stared at her and remembered his last visit to her home one week earlier. She had begun to weep as she spoke about his dead father, but he hadn't been able to comfort her. If he'd seen a stranger crying in the street he would have responded with more feeling. But he and his mother didn't have that kind of relationship. They didn't touch, kiss, or embrace, and the thought of reaching out and holding her hand filled him with dread. He would never forget the childhood memory of her passing him to Evelyn, the maid, who hugged him so warmly to her bosom that he experienced a sense of pleasure, a feeling, for the first time, of being loved. "It's me. Aaron," he whispered. But he doubted she could hear him.

He left the room and met Dora in the cobblestone courtyard behind the hospital. It was a beautiful evening in mid-October. They could see the East River with the lights of Roosevelt Island reflected in it. He knew Dora felt troubled by having called 911 and he tried to reassure her. "How can you sit in a room and let someone die? You couldn't have lived with yourself if you'd done it." But secretly he felt ambivalent. If his mother had been so depressed that she'd tried to kill herself, he knew she was going to be furious if she came out of it and had to face life all over again. And then, of course, he'd have to face *her* all over again, too. He also knew she had some money and that much of it could be depleted on medical bills. But if she died right away, he might come into a fine inheritance. On the other hand, he would have to make arrangements for a funeral. He would have to call a mortuary, place an obituary in the paper, send out invitations for the service, face all of his mother's old friends, and decide where to bury her and in what kind of plot. *How am I going to handle this?* he wondered. *I don't know the first thing about it.*

She remained in a coma for the next few days while he wondered what to do. Should he pretend nothing had happened, or tell his co-workers and his boss at the symphony? It was such a good story. His mother had tried to kill herself. She was in a coma in the hospital. It was an event. Everyone would want to know what had happened. They'd feel sorry for him. Finally, he had to tell, and eventually, as he came to tell one person after another, he began to develop a feeling for the story. For so long, his life had seemed empty, and this event had suddenly given it flavor and zest. He didn't want to use his mother's pain to get attention, but that was exactly what he was doing.

He didn't feel like eating and he couldn't sleep. It reminded him of finals in college where you lose track of time and don't know what day it is. You're haunted by the sense that you're not doing enough but there's nothing you can do because there's no way in a few days you can ever catch up on a semester's worth of work and you might as well not even bother to try. So he just went numb. He didn't want to think, "Oh, God, I wish she would die," and the only way to prevent that was not to think at all.

Every day he would walk down the hospital corridors and look into rooms where bedridden people slept, read magazines, and gazed at television. Some of the rooms were filled with flowers. He would pass recovering patients strolling the hallways arm in arm with members of their families, and then he'd enter the room where his mother lay unconscious.

And now, for the first time, Aaron could sit beside his mother and she had nothing to say. It was a strange feeling because she was a woman who, in the company of others, always held forth. At La Brasserie two weeks ago, as they waited for the soup, she had begun to sing.

Am Brunnen vor dem Tore,
Da steht ein Lindenbaum:
Ich träumt in seinem Schatten
So manchen süssen Traum.

"What is that?" he interrupted, embarrassed by the stares of people at nearby tables.

" 'The Linden Tree' by Schubert."

"What's the translation?"

She looked off and smiled. " 'Down there by the fountain at the gate stands the linden tree. I dreamed in its shadow so many a sweet dream.' "

"That's nice."

"My teacher told me I was her best student. She wanted me to attend the Conservatory. But you know how it was in those days. A woman was supposed to marry and raise children. No one cared about my career. Then I met your father—

and that was that. If I'd had the chance to sing professionally, my life might have been completely different."

Yes, he thought. *I wouldn't have been born.*

"Maybe I'd be singing at the Metropolitan now," she said. "I've lost some of my technique, but the purity and the sweetness are still there."

She sang the second verse.

> *Ich schnitt in seine Rinden*
> *So manches liebe Wort;*
> *Es zog in Freud und Leide*
> *Zu ihm mich immer fort.*

As her voice rose, Aaron began to squirm and cringe and thought if he remained in his chair one more second, he might begin to scream.

From four to midnight, the nurse on duty was a young woman from Switzerland called Helga. She had blue eyes, ruddy cheeks, and long blond hair wrapped in a braided coil. To Aaron, she looked like a Teutonic snow goddess. He liked to imagine meeting her in an empty operating room. She would lie down on the table, unwrap her braid, and let him tie her up with it.

After his mother's death, Aaron got a job singing and playing the guitar in a small Upper West Side bar. The room was dimly lit. There were nine wooden tables with candles and vases of flowers. The kitchen served hamburgers, steaks, two chicken dishes, and steamed vegetables. At midnight, when

Aaron showed up, the cook would be closing down and there would be only hard-core drinkers left.

He would hook his guitar to one input of the speaker and a lavaliere microphone, clipped below his collar, to the other. The waitresses, sitting at the bar smoking and drinking with their boyfriends, wouldn't bother to clean up, and half-empty glasses, greasy plates, and ashtrays full of cigarette butts still littered the tables. He would climb onto a raised platform and begin to sing, playing to the backs of about five or six people slumped at the bar. By the middle of his second set a ripple of late-night drinkers would come in, mostly students from Columbia University. Then, at around 2:00 A.M., somebody who had appeared to be listening intently would start to sway and fall over with his glass, overturning his stool. Or a group of people would clap and yell and begin to dance, and Aaron would think they were really getting into his music until he realized that they were so drunk they would have done the same thing no matter who was performing. There was also a bum in filthy, soot-covered clothes who used to stop by. He would stand in the doorway, bobbing his head. For the first few weeks Aaron thought he was bobbing his head to the music, but it turned out to be a nervous condition. Aaron did have a few fans, two young men in their mid-twenties who would shout, "Rock 'n' roll, rock 'n' roll," when he arrived at midnight. They had become his pals ever since he had let them join him on stage for a set one night.

There was no air-conditioning and no ventilation and everyone smoked. People smoked cigarettes all night, and the following day not only did Aaron's clothes and guitar smell of smoke, but his eyes felt seared.

The manager, Manuel, was a Chilean with the face of an old prizefighter. He had scar tissue above one eye and a broken nose. He liked to think of himself as an impresario who was fostering new talent. He gave Aaron free drinks, dinner, and fifteen dollars a night. But as time passed and he lost money, he began to turn on Aaron. If Aaron took too long a break between sets, he would come over and say in heavily accented English, "What do you want? What do you do? You come in here, you sit, you talk. How can I make money if you don't get up and play?" The bar began to deteriorate. He cut back on the candles and the flowers. He took the spotlight away and used the current for a Budweiser sign he put in the window. Rats in the kitchen began to wander into the dining area, and roaches and water bugs streamed from holes in the walls and floors. One night, Aaron saw a huge roach crawl out of his guitar and tried to kill it with his pick while he was performing. Finally, the bar closed down.

A few weeks ago, Aaron took a walk in Central Park. It was a beautiful fall day. The air was fresh, the light clear, and the trees looked as if they were on fire. He sat on a bench and watched a group of boys and girls play touch football. They were wearing Scotch plaids, argyles, woolens, and Shetland sweaters. The colors were maroon and blue and dark gray and shades of tans and reds like the leaves. It made him think of college, of the smell of new books with fresh print and bindings that break, of the first days of new classes and the prelude to winter. When he got back to his apartment, he paced back and forth, washed the dishes, stared out the window at the traffic, turned on the TV, experienced a tightness in his throat that threatened to squeeze tears from his eyes at any moment, and felt a crushing weight on his chest that almost prevented him from breathing.

One night he had a dream. It was dusk. He was in a deserted part of the city. Beside him was a five-year-old boy who resembled a photograph he'd seen of himself as a child. They were in a working-class neighborhood of low-rent, single-family homes with beat-up wooden porches and untended yards. There were no people, no cars passing, and no lights in the windows of the houses.

He had no idea where they were, but there was a route he felt he had to follow. He did not know where it led, but they had to squeeze under fences, climb through prickly hedges, make their way across yards littered with rusty old lawn furniture, cut through empty lots with weeds and piles of trash, and enter a playground, its swings gone and its sandbox filled with garbage. He pretended it was a game, that they were having fun, going on an adventure, and the boy tried not to show his fear by playing along with him. But the sun had gone down and it was getting cold.

He took the boy's hand and they walked to an old-fashioned phone booth on the corner. He lifted the receiver, dialed "0," and heard a recording. "To place a call, please deposit twenty-five cents." It was his mother's voice. At first he couldn't believe it. Then he remembered his mother worked for the phone company recording messages on tape. It occurred to him that if he could get an operator he might be able to reach her. He tapped the cradle until he heard a woman pick up. "This is operator 473."

"Hello," he said. "My mother works for the phone company in the recording department." He gave her name and asked if they could be connected. But the operator had never heard of her and couldn't find her on the employee roster. She asked what number he was calling from. He looked at the phone. "There isn't a number listed here," he said.

"I wish I could help you," she said, "but I cannot connect you with anyone unless you place a quarter in the slot."

"Look, we're lost. We don't know how to get home. I don't have any change."

"There's nothing more I can do."

"Let me speak to your supervisor!" he said angrily.

"My supervisor isn't here," she answered. "Besides, I'm acting supervisor."

He remembered when he and the boy had first gone out it had been sunny and warm. Now it was getting cold and it smelled like snow. The boy came into the booth with him, and they closed the door to keep the wind out.

"There's one thing you can do," the operator said. "Hang up and call 555-4327. It doesn't require any change. Maybe they'll be able to help you."

He hung up, dialed the number, and it was busy. He hung up, waited thirty seconds, and tried again. This time it just rang. He hung up and dialed "0," but no one answered there either. After listening to the phone ring for three minutes, he began jiggling the cradle. Finally, in frustration and rage, he slammed down the phone and the receiver shattered.

By now it was dark outside. The streetlamps were broken and there were still no lights in the windows. He decided to look for help in the neighborhood. But the door of the booth was stuck, and the harder he tried to open it the more it seemed to seal shut. The boy was pleading with him, "Don't push it this way, push it that way," when suddenly the phone began to ring. He stared at the broken receiver helplessly, feeling inept, frightened, and ashamed because he knew he was responsible for everything that had gone wrong and the boy, who was crying, would never forget it. And they huddled in the booth, a raw wind blowing outside, a light snow beginning to fall, the phone ringing and ringing and ringing.

When he was younger, Aaron ate just about everything. He was proud of his iron stomach. Then, when he was in his late thirties, he drank a Coke, belched, and felt a pain below his left breast, near his heart, as if a bubble had burst inside his chest. It was a completely unfamiliar feeling. For years he'd seen ads for Alka-Seltzer, Pepto-Bismol, and Maalox, and had felt disdain for people who had trouble with their digestion. But now, at various times during the day, he takes different kinds of antacids while continuing to eat at fast-food joints. When he goes to McDonald's he'll have a Big Mac, large fries, and a medium Coke. At Kentucky Fried Chicken, three pieces of extra crispy chicken, coleslaw, and a Coke. At Pizza Hut, a small plain pizza and a root beer. Or at Subway, he orders tuna with oil, mayonnaise, green peppers, onions, and olives on a huge roll. Then he'll go to a chocolate-chip-cookie store and buy a half dozen cookies, or stop at a Dunkin' Donuts for a doughnut and coffee, or go to a Häagen-Dazs for a cone or a sundae.

Recently, he's put on so much weight that he gets winded putting on his clothes and has begun wheezing like an asthmatic. He's afraid to bend over because something might pop or break or, straightening back up, he might see stars, go into tunnel vision, brown out. When he's sitting in a fast-food restaurant, where the furniture is bolted to the floor and he can't back the chair away from the table, the table cuts into his belly. He'll catch sight of himself in a mirror, sitting in that unwashed and unshaven state, and he looks like one of those weird fat guys in a restaurant. Passing people in doorways never used to be a problem—he'd just swivel to one side—but now he takes up the entire space himself. And he can't fit into his clothes anymore. His ties don't fall but slope outward, resting on his belly, and when he's lying in bed eating dinner, his stomach serves as a tray. He can put plates, silverware, and a napkin on it.

"The more weight you put on," he says, "the more you surround yourself with another layer, so you can't be reached. It's like insulation." He sits in a chair, holding his huge stomach in his hands. "Yes, I feel it stands as a monument to my excess." But making love has become difficult. The missionary position is now a problem because he's afraid he'll suffocate someone. And if, on the other hand, he lies on his back, it won't be easy for her because she'll have to straddle his giant belly.

A few weeks ago he was caressing a prostitute he'd picked up in a bar. They were fully clothed on the sofa in her apartment when he had an orgasm. As he got up, he saw a red stain on the lap of her white dress and assumed she was having her period. But in the bathroom, his pants and underpants soaked with blood, he realized it had come from him.

"You know, when I think about myself and the life I've led, I feel self-loathing, shame, disgust. I'm a waste and a failure," he says. "But when I imagine myself as a character in a novel . . . well, I think I'm pretty interesting, kind of offbeat, intriguing, entertaining."

Night

*K*evin vacuumed the pool. He brushed down the walls and measured out the chlorine. When he was finished the water took on a clear, bluish hue. He gazed up at the house, with its bay windows, exposed timber, and steeply pitched roof. Then he looked over at the middle-aged couple eating sandwiches at a table under an umbrella. The wife, slim and dark-haired, wore a loose-fitting sundress and sandals. Her husband, balding and overweight, wore a sweatsuit several sizes too large for him. When he saw that Kevin was ready to leave, he got up, tightened the drawstring around his waist, and walked over.

"Thank you, Kevin. Great job." He gave Kevin an envelope, and they shook hands.

As Kevin drove off in his Land Cruiser, he remembered

with distaste the time he had removed bits of leaves and insects that had collected in the filter and tried to explain the purification system to them, and their faces went blank. Neither seemed interested in the operation of the pool. They simply wanted it cleaned and maintained. Like so many people he worked for, they had no idea how the equipment they owned really operated. They knew which buttons to press and what dials to turn, but without repairmen to rely on, everything they owned would fall apart and they wouldn't be able to do a thing about it. What would happen if a catastrophe destroyed the comfortable world they lived in? How would they survive?

You didn't need to be a religious zealot to believe in impending disaster. The world seemed poised on the edge of an abyss. Tremors were recorded every week and a major earthquake had been predicted. When fires started they spread quickly, fueled by the Santa Ana winds. The fires burned off the brush on the hillsides, and when the rains came, the rocks and mud, without roots to hold the earth in place, collapsed in avalanches. A few months ago, on the Pacific Coast Highway, Kevin had sped through a torrent of falling stones and had watched in his rearview mirror as a mountain of rubble rose behind him.

Violent Pacific storms were followed by high surf. When the skies cleared, twenty-foot breakers would crash into the supports of homes, battering them with oil drums and pilings that had washed down from the canyons. The salt spray of the surf created a haze that was like a thick fog and the smell of the ocean was so strong it seemed as if you were passing along a beach when you were half a mile inland.

Sometimes the odor had the sickening taint of animal carcasses that floated to the surface of the water and rotted along miles of beaches.

When the ocean tide rose into creeks and streams, they backed up and swamped inland areas. During a recent flood, Kevin had to wade waist deep in water to buy provisions at a supermarket, using his surfboard to carry out groceries, while his neighbors piled into rowboats and motor launches sent to rescue them from their homes.

A crime wave was also in progress. Cars were burglarized for radios and stereo systems. Houses were robbed for computers, TVs, and stereos. Offices were broken into, files and records taken, the buildings sometimes torched. Gunmen fired at cars from overpasses and hillsides, and drive-by executions occurred almost daily. The police were increasingly on edge.

One night, as he stood outside a bar by the highway, Kevin saw flashing lights in the distance, heard a siren, and watched a Jaguar XKE being chased by a sheriff's patrol car. He could hear rock music blasting from the Jaguar as it approached at high speed. When the Jaguar swerved into the parking lot, Kevin leaped onto the porch. The car swung back on the road, headed toward the ocean, and almost went over a cliff when, at the last moment, it corrected itself and veered into a long, sweeping spin. Kevin watched as it crashed against a bus bench and ended up facing south on the northbound shoulder of the road.

The patrol car pulled up and an officer jumped out holding a pistol. He ran to the driver's side of the Jaguar. "Don't move," he shouted, "or I'll blow your head off." His partner, also holding a revolver, crouched behind a phone booth and repeated, "Don't move." Then both deputies fired a number of shots from different angles and one of them ran to the patrol car, got a shotgun, and blew out the rear window. When they lowered their guns and opened the door of the Jaguar, the driver spilled out of the car, still clutching a tiny pistol. More CHP and sheriff's cars rolled up, followed by an ambulance and a fire engine, and within an hour the body had been removed, the Jaguar towed away, and you wouldn't have known anything had happened except for the skid marks on the highway and the smashed edge of the bus bench.

My earliest memory is of a goat running around behind me. I drank goat's milk because I was a sickly little girl and couldn't drink regular milk.

My father owned a religious bookstore. We lived in two rooms above it. I wore my sister's hand-me-downs and kept them in an orange crate in the corner of our room.

I was pretty much left alone. I'd go to a Planter's Peanut store where they gave me free peanuts. I used to sit in the back of a newsstand where they'd let me read comic books if I was quiet. On Saturdays I'd walk to the park to watch a band play.

Later the same night, Kevin was driving home in his Land Cruiser. He was slowing down for a red light when a Chevy Nova sped around his left side, cut in front of him, and screeched to a halt at the light. Kevin tried to stop as fast as he could without skidding, tapped the Chevy's fender, and saw the Chevy's reverse lights flash as the driver threw his car into park and jumped out.

"You asshole!" he yelled. "You did that on purpose!"

"Sorry," Kevin said. "It was your fault."

"Fuck you, shithead!"

The driver's girlfriend was staring back through the rear window. Kevin waved him off. The man ran back to his car, got a beer bottle from the back seat, and threw it at Kevin's truck. It shattered on the grille. Then he gave Kevin the finger, jumped into his car, and sped off. Kevin followed him onto the freeway, threw his truck into low, came up against the bumper of the Chevy, and pushed it two hundred yards at seventy miles an hour, the car's tires smoking, its brake lights screaming bright red. Both vehicles careened onto the grass at the side of the road.

Kevin got out. "Still feel like a hero?" he shouted. He turned and walked back to his truck. As he lifted himself into the cab, the driver and his girlfriend jumped him from behind. They wrestled Kevin to the ground, and while the woman scratched him and pulled his hair, the man beat him savagely, smashing his head repeatedly against the fender. Then he took Kevin's keys from the Land Cruiser's ignition and called the Highway Patrol. Five minutes later a police car pulled up and shone its light on Kevin. He had a black eye, a cut lip, and long bloody scratches on his cheeks. An officer came out holding a gun and told Kevin to put his hands behind his head. A moment later, three more patrol cars raced up with lights flashing. The sheriff who questioned him turned out to be his former Explorer Scoutmaster, but neither acknowledged the other.

I remember once, when I was riding on the back of my sister's bicycle, I let her talk me into sticking my foot between the spokes of the rear wheel and my foot twisted around backwards. I got off the bike and dragged myself home. My ankle was bloody. I couldn't put weight on it. But my father wouldn't take me to the hospital. "You got yourself into this," he said, "and you'll get out of it." Finally a doctor who lived in the neighborhood saw me limping in the street. He realized I had a fracture, so he set my leg. I was in a cast for six months. My father was so angry about it he broke a yardstick over my back.

To pay for damages to the Chevy, Kevin got a job on weekends cooking at the Marble Inn. When he got off work at eleven, he sat at the bar, had a few beers, and played darts in the back for money. Sometimes a friend would come in with cocaine, and Kevin would walk out to the parking lot and snort lines off a mirror through a folded matchbook cover.

Once the inn was rented for a party that went on until daybreak. A rock band played music so loud the inn was shaking. Everyone was drunk. Empty bottles littered the room and people put their cigarettes out on chairs and tables. Kevin was about to leave when a man staggered in the front door, his hand over his chest, blood trickling between his fingers, and collapsed. The doorman shouted, "Get some coats," and Kevin rushed forward, grabbed coats off the coat rack, and covered the man, who now lay sprawled on his back on the floor. Then Kevin ran out to see if there was anyone on the porch or in the parking lot. As he came through the door he bumped into another man, his face bruised and his hair matted with blood.

"Did a guy just come in here?" the man asked. Kevin pushed him back down the steps. "We're closed now," he said—then saw the butt of a pistol sticking out from under the man's belt. Kevin backed off. The man turned and ran. Kevin watched him dart through the parking lot and ran after him. Just before the man cut across the highway, Kevin heard the gun clatter to the pavement. He found it under a parked car, looked around to see if anyone was watching, carried it back to his Land Cruiser, and slid it under the seat.

The next day Kevin bought a case of .38 caliber cartridges. He took the pistol to a deserted part of the canyon, lined up a row of empty cans, and fired at them from about thirty feet. Later, he hid the weapon and the cartridges in a tool box in the garage.

I ran away again and again. Once I went to Chicago. It was the summer between my junior and senior year in high school. I stayed at the Maryland Hotel on Rush Street and worked as a go-go dancer. I tried to get a job as a waitress and ended up selling bags of pills on the street.

Kevin lived with a surfing buddy of his named Mike. Two girls, both unmarried with infant children, were staying there. Mike was involved with one of them, Beryl, and the other, Linda, moved in because she was a friend.

Before leaving for work one morning Mike asked Kevin to sell a pound of Panama Red to a customer he expected that day. Kevin hung out at the house and sold it to a student who got busted later that afternoon, and at around midnight,

Kevin, Mike, and the two girls were sitting in the living room watching television when suddenly the front door smashed off its hinges and fell flat on the floor. A man with a shotgun shouted, "Freeze—police," and troopers and deputies stormed in. In less than twenty minutes they forced the girls to sign confessions by threatening to send them to jail and take away their children. Then someone read to Kevin, step by step, everything that had taken place since he had arrived in the house, including the fact that he had sold a pound of marijuana. He pled guilty and spent two months in the county jail waiting to be sentenced, living in a holding tank with junkies, thieves, rapists, and a crazy arsonist who would unroll toilet paper on people and set them on fire as they slept.

One of Kevin's cellmates was a tall, wiry man named Jenkins who had been arrested for rape. Six months earlier he and four other men had raped another inmate. The night Kevin arrived, Jenkins came over and told him he had a cute ass. Three days later, in the morning, when Kevin was still asleep, a pillow hit him. He lifted himself groggily and saw Jenkins standing at the foot of his bed with a leering grin. "Hi, cute-ass," he said. Kevin stared at him, then slowly got up.

That night there was a card game. Kevin was dealing when Jenkins came up behind him, hooked one arm behind Kevin's head in a half nelson and, with his other hand, grabbed Kevin's crotch. "I want to look at that cute ass of yours," he said. Kevin drove his elbow into Jenkins's ribs, turned, and punched him. Jenkins fell and Kevin kicked him in the stomach. Jenkins crouched on the floor, lifted himself slowly, and was about to charge at Kevin when he saw a guard coming down the corridor. "I'm going to kill you," he said.

But nothing happened because Kevin made friends with an enormous black man called Pockets. Every December, when the weather turned cold, Pockets would get himself arrested and spend a few months in prison. This winter, he had been charged with putting trash cans in the middle of the street and setting them on fire. Pockets knew everybody in the jail. He had been a trusty so many times he knew where every broom and towel and sheet was stored. So with Pockets—who was well over six feet tall and weighed more than three hundred pounds—on Kevin's side, Jenkins stayed away.

One day Pockets took Kevin aside. "I saw Christ," he said, with tears in his eyes. "He was afflicted. He wanted some money, but I wouldn't help him. Then he walked around the corner and disappeared. He could have been an angel, I don't know. But I know I failed my stewardship that night." He stared at Kevin. "Christ will come as a poor person. He won't come rich. He'll come afflicted. And if he asks you a question and you don't answer, he'll look at you and those burning eyes will make you cry."

I got a job bartending in a club where they had a female impersonator show. In a few weeks, the manager offered me seventy-five dollars to be the girl who played the only male in the company. So I cut my hair and put charcoal on my cheeks to make it look as if I had a five o'clock shadow. I wore a tuxedo and introduced the drag queens.

The men in the show arrived in business suits in the late afternoon. They went backstage, sat in front of a mirror applying makeup for two hours, and came out looking like fashion models. They were gorgeous. They showed me how to do my hair, how to dress, and how to dance. I learned a lot about being a woman from watching them.

A few months later, the charges were dropped. Kevin was released and got a job at the airport. He wore a gray jumpsuit, carried a Motorola two-way radio, and worked the graveyard shift. He drove fuel trucks to aircraft, filled their tanks, and guided planes to their parking spots and departure areas. When there was no pilot, he would move a plane with a tug, hooking the tug to the nose wheel and pulling the plane to its appropriate location. He towed planes in and out of hangars, from small Cessnas to 707s.

The runways were two-mile-long strips of concrete like giant four-lane highways. You could see skid marks where planes had touched down. The grass bordering the runways looked lush and green in the mornings, but Kevin loved the airport at night, with its white lights running along the borders of the runways, purple lights by the taxiways, and red lights for the turnoffs. He liked working there. People were going places and coming from other parts of the country. They would fly in, meet, and fly out in a few hours. He felt close to centers of power. He could see the machinery of business moving.

When a Lockheed C-5A, the largest aircraft in the world, flew in, they shut down the airport. The plane descended in darkness until it was about a quarter of a mile out. Then, suddenly, it lit up as it was landing, and looked like a spaceship. It slipped under radar netting so that Soviet satellites couldn't photograph it. Kevin could see people walking around the nose area, and they looked like ants. Then, in the dark, they rolled out an SR-71 Blackbird, the high-altitude supersonic jet. Kevin stared at it in the distance, mesmerized by its long sleek darkness. Later, when the C-5A took off, it created gale-force winds that rolled outward, buffeting planes and shaking hangars. It rose very quickly, and as Kevin watched it disappear into the distance he felt a chill run up his spine.

The next morning, Kevin tried to enlist in the air force. When they learned he had been in prison, they rejected him. But the army would take anyone. He attended flight school and was soon on his way to Southeast Asia to join the 223rd Reconnaissance Airplane Company, otherwise known as the Hawkeyes.

One evening a famous stripper came to the club. She was wearing a fur coat and diamond rings. After the show she gave me a hundred-dollar tip. The next night she came back, put a bouquet of flowers with another hundred-dollar bill in my arms, and invited me to come with her for a ride in her Lincoln. We talked for hours. Then she asked me to join her on the road. She'd pay expenses and I'd drive, take care of the car and her wardrobe.

Her name was Pearl.

Our first night on the highway, we drove for twelve hours smoking dope and playing music. Pearl had two dogs—a toy poodle and a Brussels griffin—who sat on her lap in the back while she read magazines and worked crossword puzzles.

Pearl's next engagement was at the Silver Slipper in Washington,

D.C. It was the fanciest club I'd ever seen. There was a doorman and a hat-check girl and a live band. Pearl, wearing a luxurious costume, joked and danced and stripped; everyone was laughing and applauding. She was the star. I couldn't believe I was there. I knew I'd never go home.

That night Pearl and I became lovers.

The weekend before he was scheduled to fly out, Kevin drove to Sonoma to say good-bye to his mother. Then he went north to see his younger sister Donna.

Donna lived in a rundown clapboard house on the main street of a small town. Kevin pulled up to the curb, got out, and walked up the front steps. The porch was rotted, and he had to be careful where he stepped. As he came in, two skinny dogs chained to opposite sides of the room began to whine and bark, their tails wagging. Donna's retarded son, Roy, lay on a mattress on the floor under two blankets watching television. Donna led Kevin into the kitchen. "Sorry it's such a mess," she said.

The walls were chipped and peeling. The floor was tilted toward the back, where the house was sinking. There was a Formica table with chrome legs and three chairs, two of which had no cushions. The sink had unwashed glasses in it. A grocery bag on the floor was filled with dirty paper plates. There was a hole in the ceiling where Kevin could see roof shingles and bits of sky. A hallway led back to Donna's bedroom, where a dirty sheet hung on a string in place of the missing door. A radio was playing Muzak in the background. When the song ended, an announcer said, "Nice music for nice people."

"Did you see Mom?" Donna asked.

"Yeah."

"What did she say?"

"Nothing much."

"Was there anyone around?"

"Not while I was there," Kevin said, "but I wasn't there for long."

At the end of the two-week engagement, Pearl asked me to come with her to an old burlesque theater on Times Square. When we arrived, the manager was in a fix because the other stripper had canceled. Pearl said, "Do you want to dance?" and I was hired for three hundred and fifty dollars a week as a co-star on my first night in the business.

When I walked out on stage and saw men in the front row with their flies open, I gasped and my bodice slipped down. When they realized I didn't have the greatest tits in the world, they all yelled for me to take off my gown. I tried to unzip it, but it wouldn't give. They began yelling louder, and I just got so pissed off that I grabbed the mike and said, "I didn't interrupt what you were doing, and I don't think it's very nice of you to interrupt what I'm doing." Then I threw down the mike and walked off. I got a standing ovation. The owner thought I was the funniest woman he'd ever seen. After that, I worked four shows a day.

A week later Kevin joined his unit. They flew propeller-driven spotter planes from an airfield so riddled with holes it was called the golf course. Kevin volunteered for dawn patrol because no one else wanted to do it. Each morning he would go bumping down the runway and take off, rising over a hill covered with hundreds of white crosses. Beneath them many more French soldiers lay buried.

It was a beautiful country. Once Kevin saw a tiger stretched out on grass bordering a small, gemlike pool with flowers and lily pads. The mountains were covered with dense green jungle. There were rice paddies, sculpted flat steps in the sides of hills filled with water, gorgeous to see from the sky. When the rice was tall they were green and you could see the water sparkling beneath them in the sunshine, and when the rice had been harvested they lay bare, mirroring everything above them. The blue skies and clouds and sunsets were reflected in terraced pools of liquid gold stretching up the hillsides.

There was a village next to the air base. One morning a helicopter passed over and a sniper attempted to shoot it down. The helicopter turned, came back, and for the next twenty minutes mounted a furious attack. When it left, the west side of the town was in flames. Old men, women, and children flooded the base. A woman Kevin recognized as the manager of a small bakery was carried into the hospital, and Kevin stood there and watched her die. The Americans had blown her up and tried to save her, and she had passed away without saying a word.

One night, Kevin and another pilot, Dave, drove into Sin City, a street of bars and clubs in the village. They wandered down to a brothel called the Circus of Love. In a back room, Kevin stretched out on a bed while a young Vietnamese girl wearing a leopard-skin bikini gave him a massage. When she was finished, she asked, "Want to boomboom? I pretty good. You never get anything like me." Without waiting for him to answer, she lay down and pressed her tight small body close to his. Kevin recoiled, pushing her away.

Kevin and Dave walked up to the roof of the brothel and got stoned. In the distance they could see flares, falling slowly from the sky, bathing the jungle in a ghostly yellow light, and bombs exploding in brilliant flashes. It was a gorgeous display, and the fact there were invisible human beings out there being burned and killed added a certain piquancy to the moment, though Kevin tried not to think about it.

A minute later the center of town was under attack. Kevin and Dave ran to their jeep and squatted under it, wondering how to get to the base. Should they put up the canvas top to keep grenades from falling in, or leave it down so they could jump out quickly? Should they hold grenades with the pins out and carry their weapons with the safeties off? Then they heard a shrill whistling sound and saw an old delivery truck coming down the road. It looked as if it had been built in the mid-thirties. Two men in faded blue pajamas stood on each running board, blowing whistles as if to warn people out of the way. But there was no one on the street, and the truck was only going about five miles an hour. Dave began laughing uncontrollably, gasping for breath, tears running down his cheeks. Kevin put his arm around his friend and watched as the old truck approached and finally passed them, a mound of dead bodies piled high on the back.

They didn't make it back. About a mile out a grenade hit. The jeep careened out of control and smashed into a wall. Pinned down under heavy crossfire, Kevin lay on the road beside Dave, who, bleeding from a head wound, was trying to peel the unit sticker off a piece of the broken windshield. A few minutes later, Dave died.

A few weeks before my birthday, Pearl asked me what I wanted most in the world. I said I wished I had larger breasts and she paid for silicone shots.

After the treatments, my bosom was large and beautiful and gave me more confidence. Pearl told me I looked like a goddess. But a few years later I had terrible pain, and my breasts turned black. The doctor had shot me full of industrial silicone. I had two mastectomies and they put in implants.

My first night back on stage I was scared to death, but body makeup and jewelry hid it all and no one noticed anything.

A while later, I left Pearl. By then, I'd developed my own following. I tried to pick music that told a story and to take my audience through every emotion. I wanted them to laugh and cry and fall in love with me. I'd tease them, flirt with them, yell at them, toss gloves at them, and let them unzip my gown and powder me with those big powder puffs. They really liked me. I had a lot of fans for a while.

After being discharged, Kevin drove up to Sonoma. While he was away his mother had written to tell him that Donna had stomach cancer that had spread to her liver and intestines. She was staying at home because there was no point in dying in a hospital.

It was almost midnight by the time Kevin got to the house. Donna and Roy were asleep. He sat on the porch with his mother. It was the second year of the drought. The earth was caked and dry. Ants, in search of water, swarmed into people's homes. They formed trails to sinks and toilets. There was nothing you could do to keep them out.

"I can't get Donna to eat anything," his mother said, "and all Roy does is sit by her bed watching television with the volume up while she tries to sleep. He's so rude."

Kevin went into Donna's room. At first he couldn't tell if she was alive or dead. Her mouth hung open. A stream of ants crawled over her left arm, across her chest, up her neck, and to the corners of her lips. Kevin ran into the kitchen, tore off some paper towels from the dispenser above the sink, wet them, and rushed back to her room. "You've got some ants here," he said softly, and began cleaning her up. It seemed to take forever. The ants were all over her. They crawled out of her ears, her nose, and her hair. He wiped them away with the damp paper towels and went after them with his fingers, grabbing and crushing the last of them. "I'm sorry I'm so much trouble for you and Ma," she mumbled.

After Donna's funeral, Kevin moved down to the south fork of the Stanislaus River and lived in the woods by the water. He had a sleeping bag, a few pans, a coffeepot, and his clothes. Every two weeks he would go into town and buy food. Then he would sit in a bar, drink beer until the bar closed, and get in his car and drive back to the river. He bought tuna, eggs, coffee, cooking oil, soup, chili, cigarettes, a couple of six packs, and a small bottle of whiskey.

At first he borrowed books from the library, but soon found he did not want to read, and lay in the sun without thinking much about anything. He got so still inside that when he went into town he would listen to people talking and could not imagine why they were saying the things they were because there was no sense in that kind of casual conversation. It felt strange to even say hello.

He stayed at his campsite by the river for six months. Then he rented a cabin at the end of a dirt road and got a job running a card table in a bar called the County Jail Saloon. He dealt cards to people who wanted to lose their money. They never admitted they wanted to lose, but they did. He could see it in their eyes. They were all losers. The most popular game was lowball, which was backwards poker. It was a game for losers, the sort of game people who regularly lost at poker liked to play since the worst possible hand would win. But they lost anyway.

As time passed, he felt more and more alone. He thought about the regulars who worked in the sawmills, in the small factories and the mines. They sat, talked, drank, played cards, and eventually became old bums. Near the end, they lived on small pensions or on welfare. A lot of them played lowball with their Social Security. When they lost too much money, they slept in the streets, and they died without ever doing much or accomplishing anything. One of them, an old tramp named Hardy, would sit on the curb outside the bar and sing a hymn:

> *Jesus' blood never failed me yet*
> *Never failed me yet*
> *This one thing I know*
> *For he loves me so*
> *Jesus' blood never failed me yet.*

NIGHT

Once, I worked in a theater in the Midwest that used one girl a week and played X-rated films. The janitor also worked as the comic. He'd come on stage and introduce the stripper, the stripper would dance, he'd give her a big exit, tell a few jokes, and announce the movies coming on. There was a blizzard the week I was there. I couldn't drive to my next gig, and the other stripper couldn't get into town. So I ended up staying for three weeks. Each week I performed as someone else. I changed my name, my wig, my costume, my dance routine, and my music. No one knew. Near the end of the run, when I was leaving the theater, a man who was a regular came up to me and said, "You know, you're a lot better than the girl last week."

Eventually, Kevin left the club and lived on the streets. He would go to a mission at two in the afternoon and stand in line for three hours to make sure he could get dinner and a bed for the night. Once inside, he sat in a room crowded with tired, unshaven men and listened to a forty-minute sermon. Then they all ate sandwiches, took showers, put on fresh pajamas issued by church volunteers, and went to bed. The mission was near the waterfront, next to the railroad tracks, and the building shook whenever a train rumbled by.

Lying on a park bench one day, Kevin wondered what point there was in living. He felt unhappy all the time. He remembered the pistol he had stolen after the shooting at the Marble Inn and wondered where it was. If he had it now, it would be simple to place the barrel against his forehead and press the trigger. Then he asked himself, had he really tried to make things better? The answer was no. He sat bolt upright. What could he do? He needed to talk to someone. He thought of his favorite cousin, Andrea, who was studying at Cal State Fullerton. She, too, had once had problems. He got up, walked to the freeway, and hitchhiked down to see her. He told her about his sense of emptiness, how life seemed meaningless to him, and she told him about Luke and the movement called Angel.

Andrea was an initiate. She had been given a mantra, which she was never to tell another human being. She chanted it to herself every day. Once promiscuous and heavily into drugs, Andrea had straightened out since joining Angel. She was now back in college. She told Kevin that Luke was a remarkable man who had great insight. He was a teacher, a prophet. Some believed he was the incarnation of the apostle Luke. His lectures were broadcast on radio stations around the country.

Andrea took Kevin one evening to a meeting in a large private home. The people there seemed warm and caring. They smiled and hugged each other. Kevin felt like a misfit in a room full of love. There were people of all ages, from children to old-timers, and they all seemed like a family.

At eight o'clock, they sat down on rows of folding chairs. Luke entered from a side door, walked across the room, and sank into a sofa on a raised platform. He began by invoking the presence of God. Then he asked first-time visitors to introduce themselves. Kevin tried to think of what to say. He had never felt comfortable speaking in front of people. When his turn came he stood up and said, "I feel as if I'm a radio receiver but I don't know what I'm tuned to." He was struck by Luke's dark eyes. He felt as if he were staring into a well. "Let's see if we can tune you in," Luke said, and it was as if someone had taken hold of the hair on Kevin's head. He felt a jolt.

At first, Kevin was barely able to hear Luke's lecture. His mind slipped away. But when Luke spoke of acceptance, love, and responsibility to others, Kevin began to listen. Actions based on these principles represented the highest path. To be spiritually free, you could not be attached to anything. You could love other people, but only in the spirit of detachment. If you tried to control someone through love, if you set up certain expectations for the other to meet, you were not loving with detachment.

"There is a thing called consciousness which we all share," Luke said. "We don't invent it individually. Each one of us is a cell in the body of consciousness. Your consciousness is in my consciousness, and mine is in yours. You and I are the same consciousness, the same thing communicating with it-self. Consciousness is like a river, and we all belong to it. We are drops of water in it. And there is a creator, a spirit in the universe. What does it do? It doesn't do anything. It is *all*. It is *everything*. It is both the part that knows itself and the part that doesn't. The spark of the soul that is in you and me and everyone is that little piece of God that doesn't know itself, that is learning it is a part of God. And it is your job to help all the parts of God to remember that they *are* God. That is the purpose of teachers, avatars, and prophets."

When Luke began discussing magnetic light, reincarnation, realms of mind, and the holy spirit, Kevin lost interest. But he liked it when Luke said, "If it doesn't apply to you, or doesn't seem meant for you, you don't have to accept it. You should only use what feels right. My way may not be your way. If it isn't, go find your way. We love you. We support you. Do not abdicate your responsibility to yourself and to others, but operate for the highest concern of everyone as often as you can."

When Luke finished, everyone stood up and began hugging. Andrea took Kevin over to Luke, who shook his hand, embraced him, and said, "You should stop smoking. I see dark spots on your lungs."

I had an agent in New York who booked my shows around the country. But business turned bad. To cut costs, theaters dropped live shows and ran porn films instead. I performed in clubs that were filthy, roach-ridden firetraps. Many of them weren't equipped for live shows, so I had to bring my own lights and sound. One didn't even have a stage; the bartender helped me carry boards from behind the bar and pile them into a makeshift platform. I had to walk through the men's room to get there and a drunk doing his business turned around to look at me and gave me a shower. I remember sitting at the bar of a club in Des Moines when I heard a whooshing sound and the man next to me slumped forward. The bartender grabbed his feet and pulled him behind the counter. Ten minutes later, two cops came in and started asking questions. I told them I hadn't seen anything. When they left, the bartender threw the man's body in the alley.

Kevin made an appointment for a "mind study," a personal meeting with Luke. The study cost one hundred dollars. On the day of the meeting, Kevin drove out to Luke's home in

Malibu. He sat in a waiting room until he was ushered into the study.

"You've been in jail?" Luke asked.

Kevin nodded.

"I see your lives like a fan of cards around your head. I see your present existence by the structure of your body, the aura around it, the magnetic field on which your life is played, and I see your future in the form of a seed. Let me enter the eternal mind and see what you look like."

Luke folded his hands and stared up at the ceiling.

"We ask now to be placed in the spirit of Christ. We ask for that which is the highest good for Kevin to be brought forward. We ask for it with perfect love and understanding, keeping in mind his destiny on this planet."

Luke turned to Kevin.

"When you were in school, you put things off. You said, 'I'll do it later.' You daydreamed and you failed."

This was true. Kevin had dropped out of high school.

"You say you were in jail. Drugs?"

"Yes," Kevin said.

"Your use of drugs is damaging to your consciousness. You have nerve damage."

Luke continued.

"Your mother was in the tribe of Aaron during the Exodus when the Jews wandered for forty years in the desert. While Moses was on the mountain receiving the laws from God, many began worshipping the golden calf and took part in drunken orgies. She participated, and you were the child of her iniquity. When Moses returned, the guilty were put on trial, and your mother was cast into the desert, where you were born a bastard who did not know his own father. You were spiritually lost because you had no one and nothing to believe in. You became a nomad and a warrior and loathed the life you were leading. And your life today is a way of finally coping with that life, that perspective, that situation. Your earlier life has left you scarred. This is your ancestral heritage."

Once a bar owner tried to cheat me. He held my wardrobe and promised to pay me later. I started dating him because I figured, "If I can't get my money, I'll make him spend his on me." He bought me clothes and rented me a new convertible, but it didn't make me feel any better because he owed me thousands. Finally, I came to his office and said, "You're going to pay me or else!" He laughed and said, "Oh yeah? You'll get your money when hell freezes over." So I marched out, got in the car, revved the engine, popped the clutch, and drove it right through the plate glass door of his club.

Kevin first noticed he was losing his sense of smell when he was eighteen. He had been smoking cigarettes for years. People had told him smoking cut down on the ability to smell, but he had not taken it seriously. Years passed. He would walk into a room and someone would remark on the odor of bread baking in the oven or of garlic drifting out from the kitchen, and Kevin barely noticed. In the last six months he had smelled nothing. A doctor told him there were polyps in his nose. It required an operation to remove them. But Kevin couldn't afford it. The polyps began to block the passages that allowed moisture to drain from his eyes and into his nostrils. Sometimes his eyes would well up and he would have to wipe them with his sleeve. The condition worsened at night, when he slept. In the mornings he would wake up, his face covered with tears.

The building that housed Angel's cultural center was in a valley north of Santa Barbara. Kevin first visited on a Saturday, when the group worked to maintain the house and the grounds. The day began in a conference room where work details were assigned. When Kevin heard there was plastering to be done, he volunteered. He spent the rest of the day scraping, plastering, and sanding the walls of the library.

In a few months, Kevin was admitted to the center. He moved into a small room he shared with three other men. It was downstairs, on the shady side of the building. He lived out of a trunk under his bed and became the center's maintenance man. He fixed faucets, drains, showers, light switches, door hinges, and windows.

Angel's cultural centers were opening in cities throughout the country. In order to address his followers, Luke purchased a Beechcraft King Air turbo prop and asked Kevin to pilot it. Kevin flew Luke to different cities where Luke spoke to large groups of disciples and discussed finances with the administrators of the centers.

After a seminar in San Francisco, they stopped in the hotel bar and met a young ballet dancer. Luke charmed her with stories of his childhood. When he mentioned that they were staying in the presidential suite, she seemed intrigued. Luke told her the suite was magnificent and had a panoramic view of the city.

"Would you like to come up and see it?" he asked.

"Really?' she said. "You wouldn't mind?"

"It would be my pleasure," Luke said.

The three of them took the elevator to the top floor and Luke gave her a tour of the rooms. He poured each one a glass of Chivas Regal. As Kevin and the girl looked out the window at the Golden Gate Bridge, Luke turned on the radio and dimmed the lights. Then he walked over, took the girl's hand, and guided her to the marble floor near the fireplace. The radio was playing "The Blue Danube."

"Just listen to those violins," Luke said, "like wind over water. It takes you back to another time, to a far more romantic century. Mantovani is a genius. Wouldn't you agree, Kevin?"

In the window's reflection, Kevin watched as Luke began kissing the girl's neck. She pulled back, laughing uncomfortably.

"What do you think of Kostelanetz?" Luke asked Kevin.

"I don't listen to him."

Luke removed his silk scarf, brushed it against the girl's face and throat, and ran it down the length of her arm. "You should familiarize yourself with his earlier work," he said. "I used to admire him. I also thought the work of the Melachrino Strings was outstanding. But they're really not on the same level as Mantovani."

Luke slowly eased the girl's arms behind her, held her wrists, and began to bind them with the scarf.

"What are you doing?" she said.

"In my opinion, Kostelanetz's arrangements are top-heavy," Luke went on. "The cellos and basses aren't rich enough. There's no foundation. And the violins of the Melachrino Strings are whiny and irritating."

In the window's reflection the girl looked terrified.

"Please!" she cried. "My roommate is going to get nervous if I don't get back."

"And let's face it," Luke said, "Kostelanetz conducts like a sledgehammer, whereas Mantovani's conducting style is understated, though full of genuine emotion. Did you ever hear his rendition of 'Raindrops Keep Falling on My Head'?"

"No," Kevin said.

The girl struggled as Luke unbuttoned her blouse and unclasped her bra. "Jesus!" she cried. "Come on! Cut it out!"

"Another problem with Kostelanetz is that he introduced too much of his own personality into his arrangements. In his interpretation of 'Eleanor Rigby,' for example, Kostelanetz completely ignores the ironic overtones and indulges in a sentimentality unworthy of the original composition. Mantovani, on the other hand, is much less self-conscious."

Kevin watched as Luke pinned her against the wall and fondled her breasts.

"Have you ever seen Mantovani in concert?" Luke asked.

"No," Kevin said.

The girl, her eyes tightly shut, was trying to free herself. "For God's sake, don't do this. *Please.*"

Luke put his thumb in her mouth. "I'll never forget his last engagement at Carnegie Hall," he said, breathlessly. "The air was crackling with excitement. At the end of the concert the audience sat in stunned silence before exploding into applause. Everyone rose. They were all shouting, 'Bravo, Maestro,' and hurling flowers onto the stage. It was quite moving."

By now, the girl was sobbing. Kevin stepped forward. "Okay," he said. "Enough. Let her go." He could smell her sour odor. *The smell of fear,* he thought.

After a moment, Luke released her. She walked quickly out the door, buttoning her blouse.

The two men stared at each other.

The next day, Luke spoke to the Oakland chapter of Angel. "There are people," he said, "who warn of a future apocalypse. But what these prophets of doom fail to address are the personal, though no less profound, tragedies all around us."

Luke gazed around the packed room as he drank from a glass of water. "The discovery that you have lost your way in life can come upon you relatively quickly, like a cataclysm. But losing your way is a slow, eroding process. Somehow you've made the wrong decisions which have taken you to the wrong places, places from which you can not easily retreat. It is as though having committed yourself to a great journey, and well along in that journey, you realize you've been traveling in the wrong direction. Furthermore, most of your strength has been spent on moving down this path, and you have depleted your most irretrievable resource: time. For, being mortal, the temporality of your existence is the most precious currency you have to spend, and if this budget is invested unwisely it is indeed a calamity. But it is hard for the sleepwalker not to lose his way, if he sleepwalks through life."

I was dating three men when I got pregnant. I didn't know which was the father but I told each one the baby was his in order to get them all to pay child support. I took him along whenever I had dates with any of them and sent them pictures of him as he grew up.

I had to survive. I wasn't going to take any more crap. I became a master of the hustle. I'd mingle with customers using a special "mixing kit." It was a purse with a picture of "my crippled son," a letter from my mother, who "needed money for an operation," and a bottle of pills for my illness, which, though not contagious, was "terminal." I also became a skilled pickpocket. I could take a billfold off a man in just three seconds while he was standing there asking me my name.

As the movement became more successful, relations at the center began to unravel. It had started out as a community of eighty people working toward the same spiritual goals but, like any group, disagreements surfaced. Should group chanting in the mornings continue for two hours? Should everyone be required to work on Saturdays? Some people cooked dinners. Some helped out in the kitchen. Some drove to the central market to pick up vegetables. Some worked on the grounds or cleaned the bathrooms or polished the floors. Some felt they were constantly being given the worst jobs and that a social hierarchy had developed. There were the popular ones, the not-so-popular ones, the crazies, the nerds, the jocks, the cheerleaders, and it was just like high school. And while they lived modestly, Luke enjoyed the comforts of his mansion, with its swimming pool, recording studio, and private movie theater. He was chauffeured around town in a limo, cruised along the coast in his yacht, and flew to different parts of the country, as well as to the Caribbean, in his plane.

Then rumors began to surface about Luke's abusive relationships with the women on his staff. It was said that he forced them to crawl naked on all fours while he rode on their backs and pulled their pigtails as if operating the controls of his plane; that he placed crystals in their vaginas for "deep cleansing," then tied them to his grand piano and spanked them with a hairbrush while playing Muzak to drown out their cries. He had given them solemn reasons for his behavior. He was working out bad karma from his past lifetimes. It was sacred spiritual action.

One woman's husband was Angel's lawyer. The man had devoted his life to Luke. When his wife confessed, he was shaken. He confided in his closest friends, some of whom admitted having heard similar stories from others. Disillusioned, many members planned to leave Angel. Others wept and affirmed their loyalty. Luke was the best thing that had happened to them. How could they question him? How could they possibly judge Luke when he had done so much for them, had taken them to other realms of consciousness, was the person they would see beckoning to them from the other side when they crossed the threshold between life and death?

Luke invited the leaders of the movement to a meeting in Santa Barbara to clear the air. A crowd assembled at the center.

Luke entered the packed room and asked his most devoted followers to come up and read passages from the Bible that condemned idle gossip. Then he rose and addressed the crowd. "Judge not and you will not be judged. Condemn not and you will not be condemned. Christ said, 'No servant is greater than his master. If they persecuted me, they will persecute you also.' "

When we got to L.A., the club I'd been booked in had closed down. I couldn't find a job. I was broke and didn't know where to go when a girlfriend told me about a house on La Cienega. I worked there until I developed a personal client list and went into business on my own. I'd meet johns at my apartment when my boy was away at school or after he'd gone to sleep. But sometimes he'd wake up and hear me with someone. The next day he'd ask me about it. Once he came in and saw me going down on some guy. He turned around, went back into his room, and closed the door.

A few nights later, during a thunderstorm, Kevin was told to prepare the King Air for immediate departure. Their destination was the Cayman Islands. Wearing a poncho, he jogged to a fuel truck, drove it to the plane, and filled the tanks.

When he saw Luke's car, he climbed into the cockpit. Soon he heard Luke and a few others drag a heavy trunk into the galley. The control tower was holding planes on the ground until the storm passed, but Kevin didn't tell his passengers. As the plane taxied down the runway, Luke sat down behind Kevin and drew a hip flask from his pocket. He looked through the windows, which were streaming with water. Then, as the plane took off, he sat back and lit a cigar.

"I've been thinking today of the interrelationship between all things," he said. "Climate influences the nature of plants, plants influence the variety of animals that forage on them, and animals that eat those plants influence the kinds of animals that prey on them. Did you know that on certain islands in the Pacific where there are no rats, birds become rodents? They fill the niche the absence of rats created. They tunnel and burrow. They eat grubs, prey on insects, and lose the ability to fly."

The plane veered to one side, dropped steeply, and momentarily stabilized. Luke, unfazed, sucked on his cigar.

"There will always be cooks and tailors and teachers and doctors and farmers and clerks and businessmen and politicians and scientists and artists and soldiers. These niches and countless others are being filled all the time. So why shouldn't there be room for someone like me?"

Kevin's inability to smell had dulled his sense of taste. He had been losing weight because he no longer took pleasure in eating. He thought these deficiencies would result in a heightening of his other senses. But his sense of hearing seemed to have deteriorated as well. Kevin's eyes sometimes blurred out of focus. He also felt numbness in his fingers and toes. It occurred to him that he was slowly withdrawing, that the death he had wanted was in him, and he didn't care.

She likes to take a long shower in the morning and leaves the window open so that she can see her garden. There are daffodils, rosebushes with tiny pink buds, and a mulberry tree that was a sapling a few years ago and now has branches that hang over the roof of her house. Its leaves come out in the spring, light green and translucent, followed by mulberries, which she picks and eats. In the fall, the leaves turn yellow and brown and hang on until a strong wind blows them off into the garden.

After showering, she puts on her bathrobe and, with a towel wrapped around her hair, sits in her dinette drinking coffee and listening to the radio. Then she goes outside to tend the garden. She loves not only the colors of flowers, but their fragrances, the silky feel of the petals, and the veined, grainy texture of the leaves.

Sometimes she'll go for a ride in her wine-red convertible. As she drives along narrow, winding roads, she gazes at the mountains and grasses and wildflowers, recognizes the same trees that she has seen for years, and notes their seasonal changes. She likes to pass a large country club with rolling hills, wooded areas, and greens with flags rippling in the breeze. Whenever it's rained, the smell of eucalyptus goes on for half a mile, a spicy, pungent odor she loves, and she slows down and inhales it deeply.

When she comes home, she listens to music and sits at her desk writing in her journal. Folded in the top drawer is a newspaper article from years ago. "He surprised me," she is quoted as saying. "I guess he knew flying was dangerous, so he took out a policy in my name." Below her statement is a photograph of Kevin and Donna leaning against his Land Cruiser. The caption beneath it reads, "You don't know what it's like to be a mother until you've lost both your children."

Green Cadillac

Anton was waiting at the bus stop on Marshall and Fifth. Brooks was supposed to meet him. Anton had sold Brooks his beat-up 1968 Cadillac three months ago and Brooks still owed him five hundred dollars. It was late in the afternoon and Anton was pacing back and forth getting angrier and angrier. Brooks was not going to show up. Now it would take another two weeks to track him down. Anton was cursing under his breath when he heard a voice call out, "Hey, buddy."

He turned around and saw an Indian sitting in a wheelchair. The Indian had matted black hair and long, thick, clawlike fingernails. His skin was the color of mahogany. He was covered with layers of filthy rags and a Navajo blanket.

"Do me a favor," the Indian said.

"What do you want?"

"Could you go to the liquor store and get me a quart of Wild Irish Rose?"

"Where?"

"Around the corner," the Indian pointed. "Past the pawnshop. I've been waiting all day for someone to push me down to the VA. I'm going to pick up my check but I've still got cash."

Anton sighed. "All right. But if a guy pulls up in a green Cadillac, tell him I'll be right back."

Anton turned to leave.

"No. Wait. Let me give you some money."

"That's all right. You can give me the money when I get back."

Anton began to walk up the block when the Indian called out again. "Hey, before you go, could you give me a hand and lift me up?"

"Do you want to stand up?"

"I don't have any legs," the Indian said. "How am I going to stand up? Just lift me in the seat a little."

Anton walked around behind the wheelchair and began to hoist the Indian under his arms. As he leaned forward, he almost gagged from the strong odor.

"Oh God." The Indian winced. "My asshole really hurts."

Anton walked off toward the liquor store. As he turned the corner he looked over his shoulder for Brooks. *That deadbeat son of a bitch.*

Blocking the doorway of the store was a man in an army fatigue jacket holding a small American flag. "Hey Slim," he said. "I'm trying to get a couple of dollars for a pint of whiskey. Can you help out a Vietnam vet?"

Before Anton could answer, the Korean shopkeeper stuck his head out the door and began hitting the vet's legs with a broom. "Go away. Go away. Stop hanging around the store." The vet staggered a few feet off, waving the flag in the air. "Fuck you, you slant-eyed little cocksucking prick."

Anton walked into the liquor store. He passed refrigerated cases of sodas and frozen foods. A fat black man, squatting below an island of canned goods, was stuffing a bottle of Rainier ale in his pants. He held the shelf with one hand to keep from falling over and worked the bottle under his belt. His ankles were so fat he probably couldn't lace up his high-top sneakers, and the laces were hanging open on the floor. As he zipped up his jacket to cover the bottle he glanced over at Anton. "What the fuck are you looking at?" he said. Then he lifted himself to a standing position and lumbered away. Anton wondered if the bottle would slide down his pant leg and break on the floor.

Anton could not find liquor anywhere and walked to the front of the store, where he saw bottles stacked behind the counter. Now he was standing in line behind the black man and a white janitor who had placed two cartons of tampons and four "D" battery packs on the counter. The cash register showed twenty-eight dollars and the janitor began writing out a check. The Korean woman behind the counter said, "Sorry. No checks." She pointed at a sign on the wall:

WE MADE A DEAL WITH THE BANK. THEY DON'T SELL CONDOMS AND WE DON'T CASH CHECKS.

Anton thought, *Can you believe this motherfucker? It would take him a hundred years to use all those tampons even if he was sharing them with his girlfriend.*

"Yeah, I can see the sign," the man said. He opened his wallet and shook his head. "Look, I don't have the cash. I'm in a hurry. You see me in here almost every day. I run the building down the street. Could you give me a break here, please?"

"Sorry," the woman repeated. "No check."

Her husband joined her behind the counter. "Too much trouble," he said. "Too many problems with checks. You come back with cash." He took hold of the boxes of tampons. The janitor snatched them back. "Wait a second!" he said. While the two struggled over the tampons, the batteries fell off the counter and the black man reached down and slipped one set in his pocket. "All right, fucking forget it!" the janitor said, and walked out.

Anton glanced out the window, then looked at his watch. The Korean shopkeeper picked up the remaining batteries, hung them on the display rack, and carried the boxes of tampons away. The black man reached into his pocket, drew out a fistful of change and poured it on the counter. He added two more handfuls to the pile. "I need dollar bills," he said. Then he began stacking the quarters, dimes, nickels, and pennies. The woman helped him, raking the change off the counter and handing him bills from the cash register.

Let me out of this fucking place, Anton thought. *Jesus, how long am I going to have to wait? This is the last favor I do for anyone. If it hadn't been for Brooks, I wouldn't even be down here.* He wondered if Brooks had arrived, looked for him, and driven away. Then he wondered if Brooks was standing outside the store waiting to tell him he had sold the Cadillac, was down on his luck, and needed a couple more bucks. But he knew Brooks would never show. He would never get his money. Everything was fucked again. As he waited, he began to feel he couldn't breathe. "Can I get a bottle of Wild Irish Rose, please," he asked.

"Just a minute, just a minute," the woman said.

Trying to calm himself, Anton gazed at jars of sourballs and licorice whips and Hershey's Kisses and a cup with individual cigarettes for sale at twenty cents each. Then he looked behind the counter. There was a small section of X-rated videos with titles like *A Hard Man Is Good to Find* and *Knockers Galore.* On the shelf above were the bottles of liquor.

When the black man finally left, the woman pulled down the last pint of Wild Irish Rose.

"You don't have any quarts?" Anton asked.

"No more," she said.

Anton paid her and she stuffed the bottle in a paper bag.

On his way back to the Indian, Anton saw a hooker swaying drunkenly in front of a boarded-up strip club. She was wearing a filthy UCLA sweatshirt, thick leggings that had holes near the hemline of her skirt, and what must have once been high-heeled shoes, but the heels were broken off. She wore an orange dime-store wig low on her forehead. It looked as if she had stuck each of her fingers in an electrical socket and her head had exploded.

"Wanna date?" she whispered huskily.

Anton felt as if he were passing through a forcefield of cheap liquor and perfume.

"Yeah, that would be good," he said. "Maybe we'll go dancing. Or dine at the Carleton. Great! A date! That's just what I want . . . a date with you. My dreams have come true!"

When the Indian saw Anton coming he cried, "Oh, God, *it's a miracle*!" But when he looked at the bag, he was angry.

"Damn it, I wanted a jug of this."

"They didn't have any jugs. This was the last pint."

The Indian unscrewed the cap. "I haven't had a drink all day."

"Did anyone show up?" Anton asked.

The Indian shook his head and dug under his clothes until he found a pack of Winstons. He drew out a cigarette and crumpled the pack. "My last one," he said. He put the bag in his lap and lit the cigarette. Then he lifted the bottle to his lips, took a loud swallow, and dragged on the Winston.

Anton looked down the street for Brooks. He figured the Indian would probably be getting a check for eighteen or nineteen hundred, which was a lot more than he was making at the moment. "I'd like my two dollars back," he said.

"Hold on," the Indian said. "Just let me get some of this juice down." He took another swig of the wine, followed by another drag on the cigarette. Then he reached into his clothes for the money. Anton stared hard at the Indian and felt dampness under his arms. There was a bitter taste in his mouth. The Indian interrupted his search to take another drink and a smoke.

"I want my money," Anton said.

The Indian reached into his clothes again. "Shit! Where is it? I can't find anything today."

"Keep looking."

But the Indian wasn't getting anywhere. Anton felt doubly screwed. First Brooks, now this dirtball in a wheelchair.

"Just give me my money, damn it!"

"Here," the Indian said, offering the bottle. "You want some of this? It might make you feel better. Come on, have a little. It's not French champagne but it won't kill you either. You might like it. I used to drink gin. That's when my eyes started to go. Can't see a goddamn thing now."

Anton walked up to the wheelchair. He grabbed the armrest and braced his foot against the side of the wheel. "Well, take a good look at the sidewalk, you prick!" he said. Then he pushed the chair over. The Indian grunted as he hit the pavement. Anton watched the wine run down the sidewalk. The Indian bawled. "Oh, shit, my bottle! Jesus, where's my bottle? Fucking white-trash bastard!"

A city bus approached. Anton flagged it down. He climbed on, paid the fare, and walked to the back. As the bus pulled away, he looked out the window, and saw the Indian crawling out into the street as Anton's green Cadillac slowly cruised around the corner with Brooks at the wheel.

Date

*T*hey were sitting in a bar. The room was crowded and noisy. A waitress came to their table and asked if they would like to order drinks. While he studied the wine list the waitress stared at the ceiling.

"I don't know if I can make up my mind," he said.

"Then I won't bring you anything." The waitress turned and left.

"You know," she said, "usually when I go out with men, I worry about them flirting with the waitress. I wonder if they find her more attractive than me. But in your case there's no problem. You have a remarkable uneasiness that's quite wonderful. You make everybody feel uncomfortable. It's a gift."

"Thank you," he said.

"This afternoon, I checked my chart and found something intriguing. Venus is exactly in conjunction with Mars. Do you know what that means?"

"No," he said.

She drew an astrology calendar from her purse, opened it, and began to read.

" 'This transit produces a strong desire for the opposite sex. Venus acting upon Mars, rather than Mars upon Venus, softens the nature of Mars and will make you more willing to meet your partner's needs. Under this influence, the sexual relationship will be very satisfying to both of you.' Isn't that great?" She laughed. "Would you like to hear what it says about you?"

"Is this really necessary?" he asked.

"Of course it is."

She turned to another section of the book. " 'This transit will arouse your interest in finding a partner because it represents the union of the two planets that most strongly affect the sex drive. You have a strong desire for lovemaking and demand some form of gratification.' What do you think of that?"

"I don't know what to think," he said.

"Last Friday was difficult for a lot of people because of the solar eclipse," she said. "I cried all day and all night, and every one of my friends called because they were all upset. I'd hang up—and the phone would ring again. Finally, at two in the morning, my ninety-year-old grandmother called and said, 'Live every day one at a time. And don't worry. I'm praying for you. Things could be worse. Remember that Isaac Newton's cat knocked over a candle that burned his life's work.' "

"Is this true?"

"I don't know. She has lots of stories."

"Maybe it wasn't Isaac Newton, but Irving Neufeldt."

"Who's Irving Neufeldt?"

"How should I know?"

She laughed.

He did not think what he had said was particularly funny.

"Anyway, Grandma told me that Sunday, when I came to visit, I could take Oliver home with me. Oliver is a toy raccoon I used to sleep with when I stayed over at her apartment as a kid. So the next day I was driving along Rock Creek Parkway singing, 'Oliver, Oliver, Oliver, I'm coming to get you'—when all of a sudden an animal ran onto the road. I jammed on the brakes, swerved, and almost lost control of the car. It was a raccoon. I think I killed it. Isn't that weird?"

The waitress came back to their table. She ordered a cup of tea and he ordered a vodka tonic.

She was still wearing a name tag from the television awards banquet. Earlier she had called him from a phone booth in the hotel. He could hear the crowded lobby in the background. "Is that a sound effects record?" he asked. "You don't seriously think I'm dumb enough to believe you've won an award, do you? What kind of fool do you think I am?"

"A considerable one," she said, laughing.

Then he heard someone else's voice and her excited response. "Carlos is here? Really? Later tonight?" And speaking into the phone again: "I can't believe it. An old friend of mine is in town. He'll be giving a party later for some Spanish friends. They're going to dance the Cumbia."

"I don't want to go to a party," he said. "Let's meet for drinks and you can go there later."

He stared out the window at the slow-moving traffic.

"Did you speak to your boss?" he asked.

"Yes. This morning."

"What happened?"

"I told her if they didn't want me, I'd leave."

"The same week you won an award. It's ironic."

"You're not kidding."

"What did she say?"

"She was very warm. I think she's grateful that I'd rather give up my job with dignity than be beaten out of it with a stick. She seemed to admire my attitude—and I may live to regret it. I said it would take a few months to find something else and I hoped they'd look the other way. She agreed in principle."

"How do you feel about it?"

"Relieved. Anyway, I have an idea."

"What is it?"

"I may start an improvisational therapy theater. People baring their souls before a live audience. After all, every time you talk to someone it's an improvisation, and people's lives are so rich and interesting." She sighed. "If everything falls through and I end up broke, it might be the best thing that ever happened to me."

"That's what some people say," he said. " 'When I lost all

my money, it was the best thing that ever happened to me.' Of course, those are the ones who get their money back. You never hear about the ones who stay broke. But the ones who get it back, they're the ones who tell you how great it was to lose it all."

"Tell me about it. I've lost it all already."

She filled her cup from a small metal teapot. A stream of water dribbled onto the tablecloth. He lifted the top of the teapot and the dripping stopped. "Something I learned," he said. "If you don't lift the top of these things, the water runs everywhere. Incidentally, how do you dry yourself after taking a shower?"

"I wear a bathrobe and a towel on my hair. It makes me look like—"

"Beulah?"

"Thank you. That's very kind. And this is during the idealized portion of our relationship. Think of what I can expect in the future."

"What future?"

"I know there's no future."

"When I'm attracted to someone, I can never tell anything sexual about him until I touch him," she said. "Just looking doesn't work. I really have to feel the person."

"Like holding a melon in the market?"

"Yes, it *is* like that. For example, when I first met you, I didn't think, 'What a handsome man, how adorable.' I didn't think you were my type. Your looks didn't resonate for me. But the more I got to know you, the more attractive I found you."

"I'm glad I was able to break through your initial indifference to me."

"That isn't what I said. I'm talking about touch as a channel for opening up and expressing feeling. That's why people who are shy leap into bed with strangers. It's a way to get past the initial awkwardness to something deeper. But if you just talk, then eventually you end up in a situation where you're both scrutinizing each other and emotions are throttled because there's no place for them to go." She paused. "Look, when you touch me, I feel something powerful. What I'm trying to say is that I wish I could express myself through making love to you." She smiled sheepishly.

"How would you feel if I paid you?" he asked. "You'll need the money soon, anyway, when you lose your job."

"Why should you pay me when I'd happily do it for free?"

"Don't ask."

She lifted her cup to her mouth, then set it back in its saucer.

"During my entire childhood I was never told I was pretty. In fact, everyone in my family criticized my appearance. They were always staring at me, moving my hair around, trying to get me to look better. I was a skinny, bucktoothed, pale, depressed kid—a classic ugly duckling. But then, when I became a teenager, I suddenly blossomed. There was this mounting wave of male attention, and it gave me an exaggerated sense of my own beauty. But I put a lid on that by getting married."

"For how long?"

"Six and a half years."

"Really?"

"I was completely faithful."

"Did he abandon you?"

"In a way."

"What do you mean?"

"I don't know if I want to go into all this."

"We've got the evening."

"Well—it wasn't the first time."

She looked out the window. "When I was five, my father was hounded out of his government job because of Communist ties. He was under public investigation and fled to Europe. He was away for a long time. My mother fell into a depression and they put her in a hospital. When he finally came back, she recovered. But later the same year, he became ill with testicular cancer. His testicle was removed and he received radiation. It's always been one of the great secrets in our family. Anyway, a few months ago, she came to Washington to visit. We sat down to dinner and she was in one of her worst moods, near the edge, bitterly denouncing her life. I thought I should be supportive and let her vent her feelings. Then she started discussing her sex life with my father."

"What do you mean?"

"She talked about how sensitive and vulnerable he became after the operation. I didn't want to hear it, and if I'd had more presence of mind . . ."

"But you must have been interested."

"Well, I thought the truth couldn't hurt. Honesty is good for everybody. Some bullshit idea like that."

"Is that what your Freudian therapist suggested? Or your Jungian?"

"It hasn't really come up."

"So what did your mother say?"

"She described a sexual relationship that was total misery and acted out both parts. She imitated my father's gestures and words, and how he would correct her technique. 'Don't do that. Do this. That hurts. This feels better.' And she'd be saying, 'Yes, dear. Yes, dear.' Can you imagine? This is the kind of information everyone wants to learn about their father—that the great patriarch of the family is, in fact, fearful, hypersensitive, uncomfortable with himself sexually. I watched her, thinking: *Mom is having another breakdown. I'm responsible for her.* But by the time she left, I thought *I* was the one who'd crack up."

He noticed the people at a nearby table had fallen silent. He felt himself flush with embarrassment and leaned forward.

"You're talking too loud," he said.

"This reminds me of my marriage," she said, lowering her voice. "My husband was Jewish and I haven't had anything to do with a Jewish man since. So I suppose it was inevitable that once I related to someone who was Jewish it would all come up again. We had a theater company together. That was our original dream." She looked down, tears forming in her eyes. "This is hard because it brings up lots of feelings."

"But why reject all Jewish men because of a failed relationship with one?"

"I couldn't be close to anyone who resembled Alan. I don't

want to be reminded of him. And I feel that no Jewish man could ever love me."

"Why not?"

"I don't know. Look, I'm talking around the subject. My husband was gay. And I didn't know it. He gradually came to know it. Or maybe he always knew it."

"Did it affect your love life?"

"Are you kidding? It was terrible."

"It must have undermined your confidence."

"Absolutely. It was the pits. That's why I needed to restore that."

"Did you?"

"I think so. But there were pieces I left behind. Parts of me that got buried."

"What do you mean?"

"The person who was pissed off and determined to have other relationships and to learn to feel good about herself as a woman left behind a young nineteen-year-old who'd never stopped loving her husband." She stared at him. "Jesus, I'm dumping all this shit on you. I'm sorry. It's just that—I'm not sure this is true—but it's occurred to me that, on some level, I've always wanted to be loyal to him." She began to cry. "And I always have been."

"Why should you be loyal to him?"

"It's not that *literally* I've been loyal, but that some place in my heart, I feel, is still loyal—not to him, because he turned out to be a stranger with a bouffant hairdo and plucked eyebrows, I don't even know *who* he is anymore—but loyal to whatever idea I had of the person I loved. Does that make any sense?"

"Where was he from?"

"He came from a wealthy suburban background. His mother was a neurotic tyrant. His older brother had been in and out of mental hospitals for years. His father was involved in all sorts of shady deals. They were not a nice family. If they'd been poor, he might have escaped. But the money kept him tied to them. He didn't have much of a chance, really."

"What happened to his work in the theater?"

"He's no longer in it. He works in trade negotiations. He's become a Republican. Isn't it amazing? He wanted nothing more than to be a WASP. And now he *is* one. In fact, before our wedding he and my father had a huge fight because Alan hated being Jewish. He didn't want a Jewish ceremony and argued that, according to orthodox Judaism, he wasn't a Jew anyway because his maternal grandmother had been a German who'd converted to Judaism. But he'd grown up in a Jewish neighborhood and his mother and father had been a product of that environment and every relative he knew was Jewish."

"So what happened?"

"We were married in Newport by a blind female judge."

He laughed. "I'm sorry."

"No, it *is* funny. It was like an omen."

"What does he look like?"

"Blue eyes. Sandy hair. Tall. Slender. Broad-shouldered. Long-legged. Gorgeous. And incredibly vain. Into clothes. Meticulous about the house. A terrific cook. Older women loved him. I mean, how many men would hang out and sing Gershwin songs with you?" She laughed. "He adored Fred Astaire. I know it sounds really stupid."

"When did you learn he was gay?"

"It took years. There were all kinds of signs, but I was blind to them."

"What do you mean?"

"He made friends with all these gay men because he said he wanted to show them that heterosexuals could understand how they felt. So we went to gay parties and dances, and I'd be one of the only two or three women there. Eventually, I told him I didn't enjoy them. Did we have to go? Then, one night this guy came over for dinner. Later in the evening, we were all lolling around on the sofa when he said, 'You know, I love you both so much. I love you, Ariel, and I love you, Alan. I'd love to go to bed with both of you. But if I had my choice, I'd rather go to bed with Alan.' When I heard that, I almost fainted. And that brought on several weeks of soul-searching about how we couldn't hurt this guy's feelings by rejecting him. So we had to reassure him that it was okay, and we continued to go to his parties. Then we made friends with another couple, spent a lot of time with them, and the husband turned out to be gay, too. Of course, I had no idea at the time."

"When did you finally realize?"

"Alan showed up one day in a pink shirt open down to mid-chest, his hair slightly teased, wearing a pair of oversized glasses and an ascot. We were going out for a drink somewhere. I said, 'Do you still want to go?' He said, 'I don't know. Do you?' And that was the day we separated.

He kept all our possessions because he couldn't bear to give up anything. Whenever I'd say, 'Can I have this?' he'd have heart failure. It was such agony that all I ended up with was a plastic fork." She laughed. "The irony is that I'd supported him through school so he could achieve financial independence from his parents. Once, I said to him. 'You know, I've spent the best years of my life with you.' He said, 'Well, I've spent the best years of my life with you, too.' 'Yes, but I'm a woman,' I said. And his answer was, 'Well, so am I.' It was like: Who was the better female? And as far as he was concerned, he was by far the more deserving one. It was a raw deal that I actually got to be the woman because I was so utterly second-rate at it, whereas he was superb. When the divorce came through, our witness was the man from the other couple who'd turned out to be gay. So I experienced the divorce proceedings with these two gay men, both of whom sobbed all the way through it. They were so unhappy. It was such a tragedy. The marriage was over. I couldn't possibly cry without competing with the two of them."

They fell silent. Finally, he looked up and asked, "Have you ever placed a personal ad?"

"No," she said.

"Have you ever thought about placing one?"

"Well, I could never figure out how to describe myself. All the ads seem the same. You know: 'I like walking in the woods, candlelit dinners, classical music, quiet out-of-the-way places, cuddling by a cozy fire, curling up on a cold winter evening around a good book.' "

"It *is* a problem. After all, what's left?"

"I've heard women are supposed to describe themselves as warm and slender. That's supposed to be effective with men. They respond to the warm and slender ads. And I read that women seek men who can offer three things: certainty, humor, and sex appeal."

"But going back to a personal ad," he said, "wouldn't it be interesting to tell the truth? For example, in your case: 'Neurotic woman, mid-thirties, believes in astrology, presently seeing a Freudian and a Jungian analyst, about to lose her job, comes from a dysfunctional family and remains tied to her husband of six years who turned out to be gay.' Do you think it would work?"

"You're rude," she said, lifting her hand as if she were about to slap him.

Later, in her apartment, he removed his overcoat and lay down on the sofa.

"I don't know what to say, Doctor. I'm drawing a blank."

"Take your time," she said.

"Why don't you tell me how you've been?"

"How do you think I've been?"

"I imagine that—No, it's too embarrassing. What am I doing in your apartment?"

"What do you think you're doing?"

"Who knows?"

He tossed her one of the sofa pillows and held the other in his arms.

"What are you sucking on?"

"A 1.5 Energizer battery," he said. "I found it under the pillow."

"I thought maybe it was an adapter. Are you afraid?"

"The word *fear* is not part of my vocabulary."

She turned on a lamp.

"Oh, God. Don't tell me you like light."

"I thought it might help clear up the atmosphere."

"Believe me, it won't."

She turned off the lamp and hugged the pillow. "I'm glad you gave me this."

A moment later, she got up, crossed the room, and put a videotape in her VCR. It was a class in body work. They watched a woman stretched out on a table being massaged by another woman. The woman on the table broke down, sobbing, telling about a friend who had died in an auto accident. She was angry at her for giving her life away so cheaply. Why did she have to drive so recklessly? Then she cried about her father, who had died in the same year, and spoke of how much she still needed him to love her.

She turned off the program.

"I need to practice the Rubinfeld body work on someone and you seem the ideal recipient."

"I doubt it," he said. "Besides, I haven't experienced any tragic losses lately."

They walked into her bedroom and lay down. He stared up at the ceiling. She lay on her side, facing him, her head propped up in her hand. He felt paralyzed. Finally, he rolled over and took her in his arms. They held each other and she began to cry. He was moved and felt mounting passion for her. They kissed, and with each kiss her mouth become more pliant, more voluptuous.

Later, she walked him to the door, and they embraced. The sexual tension, the awkwardness that had existed earlier between them, was gone. She was like an old girlfriend. She looked at him in an easy, knowing way. It made him uncomfortable because he did not really feel close to her.

"Look," he said. "I don't want what happened to change anything."

"What do you mean?"

"I don't want things to be different now."

"Of course they're different," she said.

"But I want the anxiety back. I want the awkwardness."

"I'm sure you'll find a way."

He wanted to hurl himself down the corridor, race into the street, and never see her again. But he kissed her gently and left.

She called him the next morning. If only her marriage had not failed, she said. She still loved Alan, but it was polluted. "I think I understand why I've pursued you in this relationship—which I'm ashamed of. On some level, you have qualities that remind me—" She started crying. "I can't begin to get into all of this. It's so unfair to you."

The Queen of Puerto Rico

Nick was on vacation with his mother and father. They were staying at a hotel on St. Thomas. Nick, seventeen, was too old for the other children and too young to feel comfortable with the adults, so he spent most of his time alone, strolling along the country roads and the beaches. In the evenings he would sit at the bar of the hotel sipping piña coladas, gazing at the Calypso band and the crowded dance floor.

Late one night a beautiful woman came in wearing a pink off-the-shoulder gown. She looked like a model or a film actress. Everyone stared at her as she made her way across the floor, and when she arrived at her table and removed her pink shawl, baring her throat and shoulders, Nick gripped the bar because he thought he might faint. The bartender didn't know her name, but said she was known throughout the island as the Pink Lady. Nick waited for someone to join her—a suave, darkly handsome European-looking man—but no one came. She sat alone, drinking, listening to the music. After a while, she left.

He looked for her in the bar the next night and the night after that. A few days later he saw her at the beach. She was sunbathing in a pink bikini. He watched her walk into the water, dive into a wave, and swim out beyond the breakers. Later, she came out of the ocean, her long hair streaming behind her, dabbed herself lightly with a towel, and lay down again.

Nick had never seen anyone so beautiful. Yet he sensed something tragic about her. He felt her sadness, her loneliness. If only he could speak to her. He sat down near her, opened a book, and pretended to read. Around mid-afternoon she folded her towel, put it into her canvas bag, and walked up the beach. At the roadside she got into a pink mini-jeep with a pink-and-white-striped cabana top and drove off.

He acts as if he were at a resort in the mountains. When someone calls he says, "So, how are you going to get up here? Are you going to take the train?"

"You're in the city," I tell him. "In a hospital."

He sighs. Then he says, "Let's go out to the pool, okay?"

"We can't. We have to stay here."

"Why?"

"Because you have an IV in your arm."

"I never had that. What's that?"

"Look. It's right next to you. See?"

He looks down at a tube running into the back of his hand. "Yes,

*they're good people here," he says. Then he gets an idea: The hospital
should branch out, open up a chain of franchises, and he'll be one
of the main investors.*

"What's the name of the chief resident here?"

"Brown."

*He draws a scrap of paper from his pocket, looks at it, and asks,
"What's he invoicing now? What's his margin?"*

Nick spent the following days searching the island for her.
He rented a bike from the hotel, rode along the beaches,
navigated through the bustling streets of the town, pedaled
slowly up steep hills into residential areas, and coasted down
the other side of the island to the harbor. He returned to the
hotel in the evenings, exhausted. Then he would take a
shower and wait for her at the bar. Although they had never
spoken, he thought he was in love with her.

The last night of his vacation, Nick was sitting glumly at
his usual spot when she passed right by him and took a table
near the bandstand. He knew he had to act now, before it
was too late. He had no idea what to say, but it didn't matter.
He rose, his heart pounding, and was about to cross the dance
floor when the musicians took a break and drew chairs up to
her table. For the next half hour, Nick watched as the group
laughed and sipped champagne. She never glanced at him
once the entire evening. He realized then that he would return
to the States without ever speaking to her.

He downed a few more daiquiris when a polite, middle-
aged man wearing an open-necked white shirt, white slacks,
and white deck shoes sat down next to him. The man ex-
tended his hand and introduced himself as Perry. He told

Nick he was president of a textile firm in the United States but spent most of his time in the Caribbean. Then he launched into a description of the geography, culture, and history of St. Thomas. Perry knew so much about the island that Nick asked him about the Pink Lady. Perry shook his head and said she was just a washed-up hooker who'd been around for a while, then changed the subject.

When the bar closed down, Perry invited Nick for a ride on his speedboat. It was Nick's last night on the island, a beautiful evening for a spin around the bay, and Nick decided to join him.

They drove to the marina in Perry's convertible, walked down a pier, untied the boat, and pushed off. When they cleared the yacht basin and came into open water, Perry leaned on the throttle, the boat lurched forward, and they went crashing over the waves. They raced back and forth across the bay, passing the sparkling lights in the harbor.

A half hour later they pulled into the dock and drove to Perry's home. An oceanfront mansion with Greek columns, it looked as if it dated back to the time of the sugar plantations. The rooms were filled with antique furniture and fresh flowers. Ceiling fans revolved slowly in the fragrant air.

They smoked marijuana and drank wine and Nick was stoned and drunk, watching television with one eye open. He wanted to sleep, but every time he closed both eyes he felt as if he were falling through space. The movie they watched starred Kirk Douglas, who played different roles and wore various disguises. There was a fox hunt and a murder, but Nick couldn't keep track of it. He could hear the waves lapping against the dock and, with his head throbbing, staggered down the hallway to the bathroom, where he spent the next twenty minutes on his knees throwing up into the toilet. Then, sweating and shivering, he made his way into a guest room and crawled into bed. And soon Perry was in bed with him, naked, caressing him, and he was too sick and too weak to even think, and he didn't remember anything that happened after that.

Last night, a nurse telephoned from the hospital. She said he refused to take his medication and demanded to go home. Soon, they'd be forced to restrain him. "Wait," I said. "I'll be right over."

I found him sitting in a wheelchair, wearing his raincoat and hat. His hands were trembling. He reached into his pocket, drew out a scrap of paper with a number on it, looked at it, and said, "I don't have a cent on me. Lend me ten dollars, will you?"

"What do you need money for?"

"I've got to get to Puerto Vallarta on business."

"It's nighttime. No banks are open."

"They'll open for me!"

I walked to the window. "Look out. What do you see?"

"What do you see?"

"I see darkness outside. The banks aren't open now. It's nighttime!"

"It is what I want it to be."

"It can't be. You can't make it day. You can't make the banks open."

His body sagged. Then he drew out another scrap of paper, looked at it, and said, "Let's go out to the pool."

*   *   *

When Nick woke up the next morning, Perry was gone. There was a note on the night table.

> Dear Nick,
> I'm sorry you were sick last night. I have to go to work now but hope to see you again soon. Please understand when I say that I think I'm falling in love with you.
>
> Perry

Next to the note was four hundred dollars in fifties and hundred-dollar bills. Nick couldn't believe what was happening. He felt fear, revulsion, shame. He left without taking the money.

He walked back to the hotel. His parents were in their suite preparing to leave. When they asked him where he'd been, he told them he had gone into town early in the morning for one last visit. Then he went to his room to pack. In the cab to the airport, they passed the beach where he had seen the Pink Lady. He asked the driver to slow down and thought or imagined he saw a pink towel through the trees on a dune near the water. Maybe she was really down there swimming in the surf.

His parents cleared customs and Nick was about to pass through himself when an officer in a gray uniform stepped forward and said, "I'm sorry, but would you please come with me?" Nick followed the man down a corridor, around a bend, and into a small room. Perry was sitting behind a table. The officer left, closing the door behind him.

Perry smiled. "How are you?"

Nick was speechless.

"I know you've got to leave, but I had to see you again. You have no idea how much you mean to me."

"I don't know how I could mean anything to you," Nick said. "You took advantage of me."

"I felt so much, I couldn't control myself. I'm sorry if I upset you."

Nick felt dizzy and his head ached.

Perry reached into his pocket. "Here, take the money. I want you to have it."

"I don't want it."

"Why not? I don't need it."

"I don't want your money."

"All right," Perry said, "but there will always be a plane ticket to come back, and I'll write you."

Nick returned to his home in Manhattan, and soon, every Friday afternoon, an airline agent would call to tell him that a first-class ticket had been booked for him on that evening's flight to St. Thomas. Did he plan to make the trip? Nick said no, he wouldn't be using the ticket.

Then Perry's letters began to arrive. He wrote of how much he needed Nick and wanted to be with him and with no one else and that Nick was missing out on so much fun by staying home. He didn't know how wonderful life could be. Perry planned to move to San Juan where they could live in a beautiful penthouse with a patio and swimming pool and have great parties all the time. If Nick would come down for a visit, Perry would buy him a Maserati and make him the Queen of Puerto Rico.

Nick answered that he wouldn't mind having a Maserati, but he wasn't interested in being the Queen of Puerto Rico, and that Perry should leave him alone because he was just putting himself through a lot of needless pain. But Perry wrote him again to say that he knew in his heart Nick really needed him, and that he should stop being so petulant and just come down.

Yesterday he was having lunch in the solarium. The minute he saw me, tears came into his eyes. He was sitting in a wheelchair, a plastic tray in front of him. He took a spoonful of grapefruit and dropped it in his milk. Then he poured his coffee into his soup. "What am I doing?" he said. "What am I doing?" Later, I asked, "Do you want any more to eat?" He looked up. "First I have to know what eating is." He said it with a smile, as if he were cracking a joke.

One evening Nick visited his grandmother, who was a collector of costume jewelry. As he looked through dozens of pieces in her dresser, he was immediately drawn to a pink teardrop stone encased in a silver pouch with a hangman's noose clasp. The stone reminded him of the Pink Lady and he asked his grandmother if he could have it. She gave it to him and insisted he also take the pair of matching earrings. He bought a thick rawhide strap, strung the stone from it, and wore it around his neck—a talisman symbolizing mystery, romance, adventure, and those who stand apart from the crowd.

He never took it off. Some day he would return to St. Thomas and see her again. It would be in the open-air market. She would be wearing pink slacks, a loose-sleeved blouse, a pink barrette in her hair. She would look a little older, but as beautiful as ever. He would make his way toward her through the crowd of shoppers. "You probably won't remember me," he'd say, "but years ago I used to sit at the bar of the Trade Wind Hotel and watch you." He would tell her about being young and romantic and dreaming of making love to her. Then he would reach under his shirt and draw out the pink teardrop stone he had worn for years in her memory. She would smile, charmed and flattered and a little embarrassed, and he'd invite her for a drink. He would wear only pink—in fact, he'd buy an entirely pink wardrobe—if only she would go out with him. "Of course I'll come with you," she'd say, and they would drive to a café by the sea and that would be the beginning of their affair.

Months passed. It was fall. Nick was about to graduate from high school. Perry's love letters and the Friday phone calls from the airline continued. Finally Nick couldn't stand it any longer and decided to get the bastard. He wrote Perry a letter asking for fifteen thousand dollars to buy a mixing console and speakers for a rock band he was forming. Could Perry help him out? A few days later Perry wrote back for more information. Why not come down to St. Thomas to discuss it? Nick fired off another letter demanding the money now— that is, if Perry really cared for him or ever wanted to see him again. Perry never answered. A few months later, Nick wrote another letter to tell Perry how much he hated him because all along Perry had just wanted to take advantage of him. Yet when Nick had asked for one small favor, Perry had rejected him out of hand.

A year passed before Nick received another letter mailed from a hospital in San Juan, written in an almost illegible hand. In it Perry said he had suffered a stroke, had lost some of the motor control of his arms and legs, was afraid he was also losing his mind, and had resigned as president of his corporation. He was terribly depressed, had lost the will to live—"I can't go forward now," he wrote—and hoped Nick would forgive him.

It took a month before Nick could bring himself to write back. Why should he care? Then it occurred to him that Perry might really have loved him. After all, why had Perry pursued him for so long? So he wrote to express his sympathy. He was sorry he had tried to exploit Perry for money, but he had learned something: You shouldn't use people. After he mailed the letter, he didn't hear from Perry for years.

Once I followed him down the hall into the bathroom. He stopped in front of a urinal, unzipped his fly, took off his pants, his shirt, his undershirt, his shoes and socks. Wearing only a diaper, he walked barefoot into a stall, locked the door, and refused to come out. Finally I called one of the attendants. The man knocked on the cubicle. "You can't come in," he said. "I have a child in here."

It was summer. Nick was a sophomore in a community college, working part-time in a fabric store. He had his own apartment in the Village. Every evening, he would put on his gold tank top and velvet slacks and take a cab to his favorite dance club. He would meet his friends, have a few beers, then grab the prettiest girl and step out on the floor. He was the best dancer and soon a crowd would gather.

One night he brought a young actress home with him. After they made love, she said, "You know, you might as well have been rowing a boat." Later, when she'd gone, he watched a steady stream of traffic, headlights glowing, pass below his window. He seemed to be waiting for something to happen, but he didn't know what.

The next week, a woman called. She said her name was Rose and that a mutual friend, who wished to remain anonymous, had suggested they meet. She described herself as a former model, now an artist and poet. Although she was a little older, she thought they would enjoy each other. She sounded pleasant, but he couldn't help wondering if this was a joke cooked up by his downtown friends. On an impulse, he decided to see what would happen. They made a date.

The following evening she pulled up to his building in a Mercedes sedan. Through the windshield he saw an attractive woman with gray-blond hair and a cupid's bow mouth. He got in and sat down beside her. She asked him about his job, remarked on the humidity, and turned on the radio. They listened to salsa music as she drove aimlessly through the city. He noticed she was accelerating and braking by working a lever that jutted from the steering column. Then he looked down at the shroud of black velvet that covered her, the fabric extending robelike over her feet. The material was shapeless, puckering at one point and sagging at another. Her hair, which had looked natural and free through the windshield, now seemed metallic, and her face was so heavily rouged and painted that he began to wonder about the perfection of her nose and the height of her cheekbones. She asked him to look in her bag for her cigarettes. He opened the clasp and began rummaging through old photos of her as a cheerleader, a beauty queen, a dancer, and a fashion model. Finally, he found a pack of Kents. He lit one and put it in her mouth. She sucked on it, her cheeks hollowing, and stared ahead.

They had passed over the 59th Street Bridge and were driving in Brooklyn when she suggested they go to a motel nearby where they could relax and talk more comfortably. She told him she would get the room and prepare herself while he waited in a restaurant across the street. After twenty minutes he could join her. She dropped him off and he watched as she made a U-turn into the motel.

When the twenty minutes had passed, he crossed the street. The man at the desk gave him the number of her room. He walked down the hall to her door, and knocked. She called for him to enter. She was lying in bed with the covers drawn to her neck. He parted the drapes and stared at a grassy field with a few dying trees. He could hear traffic in the distance. A toilet flushed in the next room. He turned to her and saw a pair of metal canes under the bed. He quickly averted his eyes. She asked him to come over to her. He said, "Just a second," and went into the bathroom. In the mirror, he stared at his face, which looked drawn and ugly. She called to him again, urgently. He tried to gather his wits, then came out.

"I'm sorry," he said. "It was a misunderstanding. I have to go."

Later, alone in his apartment, he thought of moving to St. Thomas. Why not go? He had nothing better to do. He wasn't getting anything out of school. He couldn't stand another year of it. So the next morning he withdrew all the money in his bank account—barely enough for a one-way ticket—called the airline, and made a reservation. It would be good, living in the Caribbean. He'd work on boats, go spearfishing and treasure diving. And, of course, there was the Pink Lady. He had never forgotten her. He wondered if she was still there.

There's a lady who walks the halls in a polka dot dress with a bright cherry collar. Her eyes are watery. Her breathing is labored. The last time I visited, she sat down next to him, picked up his hand, and put his finger in her nose. I pulled it out and said, "No no. He doesn't like that," and they stared at each other like a pair of little children. Then she picked up his hand again, put it between her legs, and held it there very quietly.

The first thing he did after arriving at the airport was catch a cab and drive along the beach where he had seen the Pink Lady sunbathe and swim. The cab dropped him off at the hotel. He walked through the lobby to the bar. The bartender remembered him. They shook hands across the counter. "Have you seen the lady who always wears pink?" Nick asked. "No, mahn. She gone," the bartender said. "She gone to de States."

He rented a small bungalow and found a job as an assistant manager in a canvas and leather store in town. He grew his hair long, got a dark tan, and wore cut-off T-shirts, tight jeans, and a pair of clogs so he could tower over everybody. He bought a battered old Renault and drove around the island with scuba tanks in the back and a spear gun sticking out the rear window—equipment he had borrowed from a friend but never used. He would come out of a store, lean into the car to move one of the tanks, and reposition the spear gun. Sometimes he would lift it out and put it back another way—anything to savor the identity he was developing, to make people take notice. He liked to imagine what they were thinking as they watched him.

At night, he would wear a pale-blue satin shirt—to bring out the tan—his white slacks, and dark glasses, and sit in the back of a club holding a drink, nodding his head to the beat. He would light a cigarette, cupping his hand around the flame, and gaze off into the distance. Later, feeling lean and agile like a cat, he would unlock the door of his Renault, grip the roof, swing his legs in and flip himself around like a gymnast. Then he would lean forward and make believe he was switching special dials on the dashboard that weren't really there to get the car started, and sometimes he would get out, lift the hood, and tinker with the carburetor, although he didn't know anything about engines.

He decided to grow a mustache, but even after a week the hair on his upper lip was too thin. So he began rubbing black cigarette ashes on it; later, he bought an eyebrow pencil and drew it in. Before going out he would sprinkle water on his hair so his curls would shimmer, apply a dark beige base to smooth his skin, and daub his eyelashes with coconut oil. Eventually, to offset the pink teardrop stone that hung from his neck, he fastened one of his grandmother's earrings to his left ear. Then, one night at the hotel, as he sat at a table near the bandstand, he became aware of a young man at the bar staring at him.

*And I drive by Luwkeo and the Dorado Beach Golf Course with
its rolling hills and royal palm trees, racing down the narrow cobblestone streets of Old San Juan, past the crumbling stadium and
the old fort overlooking the sea and the huge storage vats of the Bacardi
Rum factory where bands play at the edge of the road and vendors
sell mango, guava, and papaya juice, until, taking the last winding
curve flat out, I downshift with my foot on the accelerator, speeding
down the road to the hospital.*

The ferry Nick took to Puerto Rico was called *The Bomba
Charger.* He danced on the deck with a group of tourists who
ignored storm clouds moving in from the west. Soon they
were passing through a choppy sea but were so drunk nobody
cared. Nick was strutting with his hands on his hips, a middle-
aged woman in a sundress before him, when he noticed a
small boat in the distance. Its single passenger was bailing
water, waving and shouting at the top of his lungs. The other
dancers saw the boat and waved good-naturedly back at him.
Then the boat was gone.

Winter

When Max stretched out on the sofa, Jake climbed up on his chest and fell asleep. Max did not move for as long as he could stand it, because he did not want to wake his son. Later, after Max put Jake to bed, Jake felt so lonely in his room that he came out into the hall and lay down in front of Max's study. He slid his hand under the door so that at least a part of him was in the room with his father.

Max remembered his own loneliness as a child. When he was eight, Dr. Edith Bronfman had helped him get through a period of nightmares, the fear of which prevented him from sleeping. Now, over forty years later, Max felt Dr. Bronfman was the only one who could rescue him from the depression that was wrecking his life. Even though she insisted she was a child analyst, Max had persuaded her to take him on again.

Dr. Bronfman's office was in an old apartment building in Georgetown. Max felt odd sitting in the waiting room across from the nanny or mother of the child being analyzed. He would self-consciously thumb through a book of nursery rhymes or a fairy tale. But the last few minutes before his session had a deeply narcotic effect on him. The thought of telling Dr. Bronfman everything, no matter how painful, was exhausting. He would stretch out, his feet up on an ottoman, and doze off. Later, after the child ahead of him had left, and the waiting room had emptied, Max would hear Dr. Bronfman's footsteps coming down the hall. The door would open, her face would appear, and she would usher him into her office. Max would lie down on her couch, place his head on a cloth she had spread on the pillow, and stare through the window at the winter sky.

Dr. Bronfman was a short, gray-haired woman who suffered from bronchial asthma. Often throughout the hour her body was racked by fits of wheezing. She would gasp for air, then spray a decongestant into her throat. After a spasm of coughing and gagging she would spit into a handkerchief. "I'm sorry," she'd say. "Please go on."

Max talked mostly about his father, who had died during his early childhood. Max had no memories of him. At family gatherings he would ask the elders about the "old days." They described his father with reverence. He was a brilliant businessman, a man of great wisdom, the patriarch of the family. He had deeply loved his son. Max's mother, on the other hand, had little to say about him; their marriage had been miserable. Max would gaze at old photos of his cigar-smoking father trying, somehow, to remember him. He wondered about his father's gestures and mannerisms, and tried, by staring deeply into a photo, to summon the sound of his voice. It was Dr. Bronfman's theory that the root cause of Max's depression was his father's death.

Sometimes, after his hour, Max found himself waiting for the elevator with Dr. Bronfman's husband, who taught at a college in Virginia. He was squat, balding, wore thick glasses, and bore a striking resemblance to Max's father. Max felt a strange chill when he watched him puff on a cigar. Although it was a bitterly cold winter, Max never saw him wear more than a sweater and a sports jacket. Standing next to him in a hooded parka, woolen scarf, thermal gloves, and boots, Max felt faint-hearted and foolish. Once Max asked why he didn't dress more warmly. The professor said the cold didn't bother him.

The elevator operator, Samuel, was a lean, dark-skinned black man. He wore a uniform with gold buttons, gold trim on the sleeves and lapels, and gold stripes down the sides of his pants. He looked like a warrior humbled in an alien world. Max felt guilty whenever he saw him. While Samuel probably earned barely enough to live on, Max selfishly spent thousands of dollars on his analysis. He imagined breaking off therapy and donating the money to humanitarian causes—for scholarship funds, summer programs for urban youths, and medical and famine relief projects in the Third World. But of course he didn't.

Whenever Max walked down the lobby toward Samuel he would smile and say, "Hello," but Samuel rarely responded. His face remained cold, impassive. When Max got out on the ninth floor he would say, "Thank you," and Samuel would slam the gate shut and the elevator would drift away. Max did not know what to think. Had he offended Samuel? Did Samuel feel contempt for him because he considered Max a childish mental case? Max had no idea. But as time passed, he began to hate him. He imagined leaping on Samuel's back and beating him with his fists until Samuel sank to the floor of the elevator, his arms and legs twisted grotesquely.

One Sunday night in January, Max received a call from an associate of Dr. Bronfman. The woman told Max that Dr. Bronfman's husband had passed away over the weekend. He had fallen ill with a cold on Friday. His condition, aggravated by congestion from too much smoking, had quickly deteriorated into pneumonia and he had died shortly after arriving at the hospital. Max hung up, shaken. *My God*, he thought, *I just saw him*. It occurred to Max that, waiting for the elevator on Thursday, the professor had had no idea he would be dead in seventy-two hours.

Max went to the funeral. He sat in one of the last rows of the chapel. He wanted Dr. Bronfman to know he had come to pay his respects, but he did not want to intrude on her grief. He saw her enter from a side door, supported under both arms by members of her family. She held a handkerchief to her face, sobbing. In his disturbed state, Max could barely follow the eulogies. After the funeral, to keep his mind occupied, he went to a movie. The film was about a man, trapped in a boring and unsatisfying marriage, who staged his own death in order to begin a new life far away.

When Max's therapy resumed, only a week later, Dr. Bronfman looked like a broken old woman. Max expressed his sorrow at what had happened. Was it perhaps too soon for her to begin again? She said no, the best thing for her now was to work. Max thought about her husband, buried in his coffin, and wondered what he looked like stretched out, dead. Occasionally he would hear Dr. Bronfman blow her nose. He assumed she was crying silently behind him.

During the days that followed, Max was plagued by thoughts about the professor's body. Were his fingernails growing? Was his beard sprouting? Had his skin turned black? Would his stomach split open like rotten fruit? How long would it take before insects and worms got to him? And what was it like for Dr. Bronfman, lying alone in bed at night knowing she would never be able to touch or speak to him again? When Dr. Bronfman asked Max what he was thinking, he said he would rather not talk about it. She told him there was no point in continuing treatment if he refused to speak freely. But how, Max wondered, could he share such thoughts with a grieving widow? And by trying to withhold them, they took control of him. No sooner would he lie down on the couch than he would see her husband's body decomposing, Dr. Bronfman's face stained with tears on her pillow at night. He talked about the political infighting and illicit love affairs at his office, but it was clear he was holding something back. Dr. Bronfman insisted he tell her what was on his mind. He was wasting his money if he didn't.

At last Max broke down and described his obsessions. He thought that by relieving himself of these ideas, he could get back on the track of his analysis. But it did not work. He felt driven to repeat over and over again these images. Finally,

Dr. Bronfman said, "We are at an impasse. Your obsession about my husband is inhibiting treatment. It seems useless to continue under these circumstances."

That night, when Max came home, he went into the study. He opened a desk drawer and stared at his old pistol. He had bought it during the riots that followed the King assassination. As the upheaval spread from city to city, he believed there would be a reign of terror, the country overrun by armies of the vengeful urban poor. It would usher in a dark age more terrifying than any period in history.

He closed the drawer and walked down the hall to his son's room. He gazed at Jake's face, still and peaceful and quiet as a painting. *When he's asleep*, Max thought, *he looks like an angel.* The blanket around Jake's body rose and fell with his breathing. When Jake began to whimper, Max woke him and told him it was only a dream. Jake fell back to sleep again, one of his hands sticking out from under the covers, palm up, fingers slightly curled, each finger like the petal of a flower.

The Decline of Spengler:
A Radio Play

1

*H*offman died today during surgery to remove fatty deposits
from his thighs. I remember when we first met on the flight
from Palestine. Gazing about us at smug, well-dressed tourists
with expensive cameras, digital watches, calculators, and elec-
tronic beepers, we agreed that science had deprived most of
the world of its gods, religions, its sense of meaning and
permanence. Dostoevsky, Hoffman added, had seen the emptiness inherent in atheistic materialism and had opposed advances in technology that would "lull the human soul into a
sleep of material comfort, thus depriving it of a tragic sense
of life."

I looked out the window. Light and dark came out of the

sky, I said. The sun, the moon, and the stars made their way across it. Nourishing rain fell from it. Rainbows glorified it. The awe with which ancient peoples had looked upon these phenomena was reflected in their religions. Rooted to the ground, they saw the sky as the home of angels and gods. I recalled Elijah ascending in his chariot of fire; Icarus, his wings beating, rising heavenward. We looked back at the other passengers, who were reading catalogs, listening to cassette players, playing cards, and talking . . . and we drank a toast to the past.

Precooked chickens in wine sauce were served. We ate them gazing at the stewardesses, who were glamorous and friendly. They brought us desserts, mints, coffee, magazines, pillows, and blankets. They smiled, leaning over us as if we were their children, whom they cared for with a steadfast, though indiscriminate, love. When one of them went into a bathroom, Hoffman unfastened his seat belt and followed her. As she unlocked the cubicle, he forced his way in, closing the door behind him. He was bored, he told her, and lonely, too. In the brief struggle that followed—against a background of canned music—her arm dropped out of its socket, her head fell off, and he found himself holding a starched empty uniform, screws, nuts, bolts, coils of tubing and electrical wiring scattered on the floor. He hurriedly cleaned up, stuffing everything into the towel dispenser . . . then returned to his seat, shaken.

Later, we were told it was time for the evening movie: a popular children's adventure set in Berlin in 1936. The lights dimmed. People adjusted their headphones. I tilted my chair back, closed my eyes, and tried to sleep . . .

I heard a fist beating on the front door and lifted myself from the bed. I put on my robe and slippers and, with the oil lamp in my hand, made my way into the foyer. I was exhausted. But I was the only doctor in the district and had no choice but to answer the door, hitch up my team of horses, climb into my wagon, and ride, sometimes for days, through a labyrinth of cobblestone roads until I finally reached my journey's end. And by that time the patient had usually died and been buried so long ago that he was now but a dim memory.

I unbolted the door. Before me stood a man in livery. A few words were spoken, and I hurried back into the bedroom to change into my clothes. Soon I was racing along in a carriage. I could hear a whip cracking and the cries of the coachman urging the horses on. As we began the ascent into the hills I looked back, as if for the last time, at the sleeping village. "An operation must be performed tonight." What had the coachman meant? I was bewildered yet felt, somehow, a sense of elation.

The carriage passed over a bridge and drew to a halt in front of a palace. I was led through the entrance, down a long corridor, and up a marble staircase. The coachman halted at an engraved oak door. He knocked. A feeble voice called for us to enter. I walked into the room. An old man was lying in a huge, canopied bed. He was bald, toothless. His fingers trembled with palsy. He looked up at me with a not unfriendly smile. Then he lifted a rag and retched into it. I put my satchel down beside the bed and called for a basin of warm water. The old man reached into the bag, drew out my surgical instruments one by one, and stared at them with fascination. Then the coachman told me to take off my clothes.

2

Hoffman's funeral was modest. A few people came to the chapel for a brief eulogy, then drove out to the cemetery. Earlier in the day, I'd visited Hoffman's apartment. In his journal I'd found a map of Florida with Xs marking spots where, according to different legends, the Fountain of Youth might be hidden. The Everglades, Fort Lauderdale, and Dreamland, the amusement park in Orlando, were cited. I'd also read Hoffman's notes on the latest advances in organ transplants, deep freezing, and high-speed space travel to prolong life. I was surprised. I'd had no idea of Hoffman's obsession. We gathered around the grave, by the ocean. I gazed out at the old people on the beach.

BORIS. Nice day, huh?

JACOB. Last week there was a wonderful day.

BORIS. What day was that?

ESTHER. Wednesday.

JACOB. Yes, Wednesday.

BORIS. There was no day last week that was nice.

JACOB. Not a cloud in the sky.

ESTHER. Did you sit outside?

BORIS. Too cold.

ESTHER. It wasn't too cold on Wednesday. I know that.

BORIS. You don't know anything. Now *this* week—today—this is a . . .

ESTHER. . . . Yes, this is what you call a perfect day.

THE DECLINE OF SPENGLER

The morning after Hoffman's funeral, I boarded a boat for a tour of the Everglades. We made our way slowly through a bubbling, frothing swamp choked with vegetation, great winged lizards hovering above us. We passed villages of semi-submerged dwellings where Indians sat in water up to their shoulders baking bread and assembling parts of tropical fish. Others tended herds of sheep and cows. But this was very difficult in the swamp, entire families engaged in treading water and holding animals above their heads to prevent them from drowning.

A few days later, I took a bus to Fort Lauderdale, the second location marked on Hoffman's map. I arrived during the Aryan Convention. The hotels were filled with European and American delegates. The theme of the conference was the evolving history of Western civilization. I attended lectures, exhibitions, and meetings. Each evening's entertainment was memorable: Monday night it was the New York Philharmonic; Tuesday evening, the Royal Shakespeare Company; Wednesday, the entire Ringling Brothers and Barnum & Bailey Circus performed; Thursday, the Ice Capades; and, on Friday, the highlight of the series, an epic film of Alpine vistas, with stretches of fragrant pine trees . . . picturesque farmhouses and chalets . . . cattle grazing in open meadows . . . fields of flaming Alpine flowers . . . and lakes whose perfect, glasslike surfaces reflected towering mountain peaks. The film went on for hours, but no one was allowed to leave.

The following day was devoted to a demonstration of weapons. A bomb went off, and the next thing I knew it was dusk, I was lying on a merry-go-round in Miami Beach, my pockets had been turned inside out, and I was wearing a pair of fishnet stockings and pumps.

DR. ARNOLD. First, we prescribe a diet of foods that do not coagulate the blood . . . fruit juice . . . raw vegetables . . . clear soups . . . "fast-moving foods," we call them—as opposed to fast foods, which, of course, we frown on. Then, we place a male patient and a female patient in the human centrifuge, fill them chock full of fast-moving foods, and ask them to seek fulfillment in each other as the centrifuge revolves. And we have found that the combination of fast-moving foods and centrifugal force clears not only their blood vessels and arteries, but also their nasal passages, the pupils of their eyes, and their hair seems to take on a remarkable, lustrous quality. Now, although this lasts only for as long as they're *in* the centrifuge, some patients become mildly addicted to centrifugal activity. In fact, a few houses have been built that are revolving modules in which one gets accustomed to living with constant centrifugal force.

A murder has been committed. The trial is in progress. I prosecute the case myself. The evidence—a cup of vinegar, some thorns, fragments of wood, a few nails, and a pair of sandals—lies on a table in the courtroom. I cross-examine four witnesses. Each presents damaging testimony against the defendant, who, wearing a black hat and a caftan, studies a legal tome. But it isn't the defendant's scholarship that disturbs me. Rather, it is the jury—a motley group of shamans, sorcerers, prophets, and holy men—each one awaiting trial on charges of murder himself. Every morning they are led into the courtroom chained together. They have the wasted, faraway look of fanatics. To make matters worse, the judge seems to have withdrawn into his own world. Every few minutes he looks up, inquires as to the correct time, asks to be reminded of the general nature of the case before him, and calls a recess to have the plastic bag attached to his body flushed out. The attending nurse rolls his wheelchair from the room.

That night, at the dinner table, I don't know what to do. I'm trapped in a nightmare. The case is hopeless. The months of interviews, of compiling evidence, of exhaustive research, have been in vain. I sip my soup and eat two spongy dumplings. After swallowing them with difficulty, I bend over to pick up the napkin that has fallen from my lap—and notice my father sprawled in the hallway between the bedroom and the kitchen. His pajama pants have been drawn down to his ankles, and lying beside him is a pair of pruning shears. I can barely stifle my laughter.

3

See her every day. Plump figure. Wears too much makeup. Struts around pool in bikini and spiked heels. About fifty. Husband, former scholar, suffered stroke, paralyzing one side of face and body. Once pompous, he's grown meek since his illness. Speaks humbly now, sputtering from a corner of his mouth. Watching bubbles of saliva bursting on his lips, I feel the urge to break into gales of laughter. I grit my teeth.

She's friendly. Kisses me whenever we meet, her lips lingering. Plies me with questions about Hoffman's monographs and early plays. Where did he get his ideas? What was he going to write next? Then she tells me stories of their encounters, during which I feel constrained to laugh,

twisting my face into a smile, my lungs mirthlessly exploding air.

One afternoon, standing at my window overlooking the
pool, I watch her perform the Australian crawl. She swims
slowly and self-consciously, her hands gently dipping in the
water. She climbs out, sits on the steps at the shallow end,
and removes her cap. Her dyed blond hair bursts out, tumbling
down to her shoulders. She tilts her face to the sun, then
stretches—a lithesome, catlike uncoiling—and notices me.
We stare at each other.

A few minutes later, still wearing her bikini, she stands in
my doorway smelling of a perfume that makes my knees go
weak. Gazing at her through undulating waves of heat, I think
she's describing the onset of fever. She tells me her glands
are swollen, and I stare, distracted, at her bosom.

A few nights later, I see her kneeling before her husband's
wheelchair in the moonlight, bathing his feet in her tears,
wiping them off with strands of her hair, kissing them and
anointing them—*but with what?* I try to read the label on the
bottle, but can't make out the words scrawled in a microscopic
script. I reach in my pocket for my glasses but succeed only
in cutting my finger on the jagged edge of a lens.

There's a beach on the Gulf Coast scattered with fossils,
where you can find saber-toothed tiger remains, parts of mas-
todon skulls, ancient shark teeth. The retired people go out
on the sand at dawn to collect them. It's their consuming
passion to find old bones. They save them, catalog them, look
them up in books to figure out what they are, photograph

them, mail the photographs back and forth, write learned notes, form societies.

BORIS. It must be at least ninety today.
JACOB. Yeah, the humidity is high.
BORIS. See the sweat on the plants? That's how you can tell. When the plants start to sweat.
JACOB. I didn't say they were rain clouds, Boris. I said the humidity—
BORIS. Are you deaf? I'm telling you that sometimes it can be a perfectly clear day and there will be high humidity . . . that's all I'm saying.

4

I woke up in a study. The walls were lined with rows of old manuscripts and ancient scrolls. A lamp on the desk glowed dimly. I lifted myself from the floor and walked to the window. In the reflection I saw a bearded, middle-aged man with earlocks, wearing a black coat and hat. What's going on? I thought. What's happened to me? I threw the hat across the room and tugged at my beard, a shower of flaky crumbs falling at my feet, but it would not come loose. Then I ran toward the bathroom, unbuttoning my coat, hoping to find a razor. The voice of my housekeeper, Hilda, brought me back to my senses. "Just slide it under the door," I called.

The letter was terse. The camps—steadily filling up—were at the bursting point. I'd been commissioned to design the new chambers and adjoining furnaces. The blueprints were long overdue. There was no more time to be wasted. I must, therefore, catch the next train for headquarters with whatever designs I'd completed, or face dismissal and a departmental trial. The letter was signed by Kummel himself. I read it over again and dropped it in the wastebasket. Then I changed into my uniform and had Hilda call me a cab.

The train was thirty minutes early—an example, I thought, of efficiency raised to the level of paradox. The men of the railroad should be congratulated for their devotion to the future.

The car was crowded with men, women, and children who were wedged in so tightly that no one could move. I listened to the hum of their conversation, which seemed in an ancient, guttural tongue, and stared uneasily through the mist of cigarette smoke.

The rhythmic clicking of the rails made me drowsy. I congratulated myself on having found a safe niche in the corner, on the floor, which was covered with straw and random mounds of manure. It was an outrage, of course, that commuter service should deteriorate to this level. Then it occurred to me that I didn't know where I was going. I couldn't remember, either, when I'd boarded the train. I'm losing my mind, I thought. I'm so far gone that I've taken to boarding trains bound for districts in which I don't live. And as if that weren't bad enough, I've selected an overcrowded car with no windows, with straw for seats, and piles of dung that are attracting horseflies by the dozens.

I woke up in a shower room. I was sprawled in an entangled pile of bodies. I peered out and saw a young man loading a wheelbarrow with the dead. I allowed myself to be tossed, like a doll, into the barrow. With my arm trailing in the dirt, I enjoyed the bumpy ride to the trench. It reminded me dimly of wagon rides in childhood. I was dumped on a heap of corpses, then searched for a familiar face, a friend or an acquaintance. I saw the violinist, Jakov, lying nearby, his arms and legs twisted grotesquely. Next to him I recognized a streetcar conductor with whom I'd sometimes talked on my way to work. The man, after pleading with the guards, had been allowed to keep his cap, which was still set at a rakish angle on his head. There didn't seem to be anyone else I knew, except for the fat man who resembled Rothstein, the financier, rumored to have had affairs with famous actresses and opera singers. He looked flushed and bloated, as if he might burst. I began to search for Rachel, my former neighbor Holstein's wife. Sometimes in the drawing room of her husband's apartment we'd flirted together. It had come to nothing. But I'd always wanted to see her naked. I scanned the bodies but could not find her.

That night I climbed over the side of the trench and escaped. I traveled north, toward the Alps. Weeks later, I arrived at the retreat of the Redeemer, the Chosen One. When night fell I climbed over the wall, cut through barbed wire, crawled past machine gun nests, artillery, and antiaircraft installations. In the backyard I found the Messiah planting trees in the moonlight.

MESSIAH. Here, give me a hand.

DON'T STAND THERE! YOU'RE STEPPING ON ONE OF MY SEEDS! WATCH WHAT YOU DO, YOU FOOL!

Forgive me. You look awful. What's happened to you? You look as if you haven't slept for days.

HOW DARE YOU APPEAR BEFORE ME IN THESE RAGS? LOOK AT YOURSELF! IT'S A DISGRACE! IT'S OUTRAGEOUS!

I'm sorry. I forgot you came here on your own, through all these endless obstacles. I apologize. At times, even I am only human.

DR. ARNOLD. We have found that the soil here in Palm Beach is remarkably conducive to all kinds of growth. A patient buried up to his neck in a small garden, for example, his scalp carefully watered and tended—

DR. AINSLEY. We have also buried people—although not in that way. We have buried them head first and found that people will relax in garden soil. I think you've stumbled upon something you didn't realize: that people will relax in soil.

DR. ARNOLD. Yes. This is true. They become particularly peaceful, and while hair growth does occur, it is not just limited to the scalp. I might add that loss of hearing has nothing to do with the soil itself. It happens because by the time people reach the age of sixty, they've heard enough. So rather than being a symptom of physical deterioration, it's really much more emotional. It's people saying, "I'm not going to listen anymore because everything I hear upsets me."

5

I read Hoffman's journal every night. The first entry of Book III began with the question: "I wonder what they'll think of this?" And what *did* I think of it? I didn't know. It was the outline for a play.

THE LOST MAN

The production takes place in a church. The atmosphere is heavily religious—resounding organ music, heavy odor of incense, a collection box passed from bench to bench.

Act I

The curtains part and we find Poole, the film critic, tossing fitfully in his bed. Unable to sleep, he lifts himself wearily and walks to his desk. He sits down and thumbs through an old review. Gazing dully at it, he's startled by the whistle of a passing train.

The curtains close. Act I has been completed in just forty seconds. During the intermission, the audience is served bitter herbs, unleavened bread, and sacramental wine. While the food is handed out and eaten, the actor who plays the part of Poole enters the church unnoticed, finds an unoccupied seat, and falls asleep.

Act II

Poole awakens, now a member of the audience that just observed him on stage. He yawns, stretches his arms, and sighs. The house lights dim, the curtains part, and a movie is projected on a screen.

The film is about a man who has lost his memory. Waking up in a field one summer afternoon, wearing only a gown and a pair of sandals, he cannot recall anything about his past.

MAN. Who am I? What is this place? Peasant woman, have you ever seen me before?

PEASANT WOMAN. What? You? No.

MAN. I don't look familiar to you?

PEASANT WOMAN. No, I don't think you ever came through these parts before.

MAN. Thank you. Maybe I'll try down in the valley.

He makes the rounds of local police stations and missing persons bureaus, vainly looking through files of photographs to identify himself. Then he wanders across the countryside, moving from village to village, stopping people who look vaguely familiar to ask them if they recognize him.

MAN. I was wondering. Do you know who I am?

SHOPKEEPER. No, who are you, anyway?

MAN. Well, that's exactly the problem.

SHOPKEEPER. You don't know who you are?

In the course of his travels, he has a series of adventures with lepers and cripples, all of whom he manages to cure with the hem of his skirt.

HANS. *(Ringing bell)* Make way. Lepers. Beware.

MAN. Excuse me. Do I look familiar?

MARIE. No, I'm sorry.

HANS. I don't think I've seen you before, either.

MAN. *(Sighs)* Bless you both.
(Harp glissando)
HANS. What's happened?
MARIE. Look, Hans! Your nose—it's coming back!
HANS. Marie, your scars are gone. You look so beautiful.
Oh, thank you, sir.
MARIE. Thank you kindly.
HANS. It's a miracle!

Finally, sitting on a fence at the edge of a dirt road, he reviews his situation. He does not know his own name. He does not know where he came from. He does not know where he is going. And he does not know, moreover, what he is doing in this dismal film, so heavily symbolic, its themes of alienation and estrangement, with religious overtones, so painfully obvious.

MAN. There must be another way to solve my problem. All right. I know what to do.
(He shakes his head, disgusted, and steps out of the screen).
MAN. Ladies and gentlemen. I can't explain now. I'm sorry to disturb you. But I had to leave that film.

He walks up the aisle toward Poole. Poole is suddenly terrified. He's just seen art impinge itself on reality. He stands, draws out a Luger, and fires.
The man moans, crumples to the floor, and dies. Poole looks down at the body, which seems to be deflating, blood running from its mouth.

POOLE. *What have I done?*

Poole races out to the lobby and dashes up a marble staircase to the projection room. The scene is televised and relayed to the audience through monitors above the stage. The projectionist, a little boy with pink cheeks and wings, looks up from his magazine.

POOLE. Excuse me, little boy—

BOY. Oh, mister. You're not supposed to be here.

POOLE. —Can you please stop this film and run it backwards?

BOY. Huh?

POOLE. You've got to reverse the film! It could suck him back into the screen and bring him back to life!

BOY. Gee, mister, I don't know what to do.

POOLE. What do you mean, you don't know what to do? Aren't you the projectionist?

BOY. Sure, but . . .

POOLE. Is there a supervisor or somebody?

BOY. Do you want to talk to the manager?

POOLE. Yes, the manager. Where is the manager?

BOY. Oh, he's in the manager's office.

POOLE. Well, where *is* the manager's office?

BOY. You step out in the hall. Make your first left. Go up the flight of stairs. It's about the fourth door—

Poole rushes out and begins running up the spiral staircase. Gasping, he finally reaches the door of the manager's office. He knocks. There's no answer. He tries the knob and the door swings open. The room smells of decay. Poole plunges forward, his hand clasped over his mouth and nose, until he comes upon the carcass of an old man sprawled on the floor, his eyes and mouth open.

Downstairs in the theater, the curtains close. A small crowd forms around the body, which still lies in the aisle. Someone breaks down sobbing, another cries shrilly for an ambulance, a third runs out to the lobby yelling, "Find a phone and call the police!" Each one, however, is an actor playing a role. The audience, now assured that positive action is being taken, settles down to the last act.

Act III

We find Poole hermetically sealed in a phone booth. He dials numbers and speaks to people, but we can't hear anything he says. Perhaps he's consulting his lawyers. Perhaps he's speaking with members of his family. Perhaps he's dialing at random and conversing with anyone who will talk to him. The audience is left in doubt. We can only watch his facial expressions and gestures, his mouth shaping the contours of words we can't quite make out. During Poole's dumb show, a heated discussion progresses on center stage. The panel is composed of robed clergymen who debate the responsibility for Christ's death.

FATHER BLUNT. Was Christ's martyrdom genuine, since he rose again? It is a difficult question in law.

BROTHER THEOBALD. Well, truly, in lines 31-57 it says, "Though He rise again, be He still dead, among us He shall walk." So you see it's not born into the man as he will be risen later, but actually as he rises himself, he proves himself.

The argument soon gets derailed, sliding into tangential questions concerning celibacy, priestly habit, the superiority of certain wines.

FATHER BLUNT. The ideal has always existed.

BISHOP BOYLAN. Ah, yes. But the ideal has no meaning anymore. Practice is all. What are we here for if not to practice?

BROTHER THEOBALD. Brothers, this is not a discussion of Platonic concepts.

BISHOP BOYLAN. Precisely.

BROTHER THEOBALD. It's not a question of the caves. This is a question, if a man be risen, can he be said to be a martyr?

BISHOP BOYLAN. Yes, Doctor O'Malley was right when he said that martyrs cannot exist if they do not enter into the mainstream of civilization. So, when we are spoken of as men of the cloth, I think the tailoring of our habits should be considered as important as the tailoring of our ideals.

BROTHER THEOBALD. Man is known by the raiment he doth put on.

FATHER BLUNT. Indeed. It is what they called *illustratio ex vestitu*. Or, if you will, *vestitus sine vestitu* in the case of one who goes without cloth. So we must be with the cloth and of the cloth—

BISHOP BOYLAN. Yes, by the cloth, of the cloth—

BROTHER THEOBALD. And through the cloth I think we shall succeed.

BISHOP BOYLAN. My goodness, just look at you! There are wine stains all over your cassock! It's an abomination! Why in the world don't you get those wash-and-wear cassocks we've spoken of so often?

BROTHER THEOBALD. Father, I'm not so vain as to—

BISHOP BOYLAN. You are a pig.

BROTHER THEOBALD. You are an idolator!

FATHER BLUNT. You can't tell a Châteauneuf-du-Pape from sherry.

BISHOP BOYLAN. A Châteauneuf-du-Pape is a very sarcastic wine with a terribly bitter aftertaste and a not very confident bouquet.

BROTHER THEOBALD. A wine of very small nose and of presumption.

BISHOP BLUNT. I take offense—

BROTHER THEOBALD. It has no finesse!

The audience, at first intrigued but now bored, begins to file out of the theater. The remaining few are rewarded for their patience with an organ recital. The music drowns out the clerics, who, unable to reason any longer, engage in a violent struggle for dominance. Poole bursts out laughing. Perhaps he has just heard something witty over the phone. Perhaps he is amused by the priests' slaughter. Perhaps he is laughing at the awful silence of the universe. We watch him grip his belly, his body bent forward, shoulders jerking convulsively, tears streaming down his face—which is buried now in his cupped hands—as the curtain slowly closes.

SICK WOMAN (through telephone). Hello.

DOCTOR AINSLEY. Hello.

SICK WOMAN. Doctor, listen.
DOCTOR AINSLEY. Yes.
SICK WOMAN. I'm wearing a neck brace.
DOCTOR AINSLEY. Yes.
SICK WOMAN. I had a freak accident.
DOCTOR AINSLEY. Uh huh.
SICK WOMAN. When I bent down. And my bones are twisted on the left side.
DOCTOR AINSLEY. Uh huh.
SICK WOMAN. I'm on Valium all the time.
DOCTOR AINSLEY. Yes.
SICK WOMAN. Because I have fast heartbeats of a hundred and thirty-five beats a minute.
DOCTOR AINSLEY. Yes.
SICK WOMAN. Which means my heart could burst and I could drop dead of a heart attack.
DOCTOR AINSLEY. Well, what exactly is the problem?
SICK WOMAN. It's . . . ahh . . . breathing . . . heavy on the chest.
DOCTOR AINSLEY. Uh huh.
SICK WOMAN. And a very nervous stomach.
DOCTOR AINSLEY. Yes. Go on.
SICK WOMAN. And I start to sweat and feel hot when it's not.
DOCTOR AINSLEY. Uh huh.
SICK WOMAN. And I feel cold when it's not.
DOCTOR AINSLEY. Uh huh. Yes. Go on.
SICK WOMAN. And I think like I'm dying and I wish I would die to end it all.
DOCTOR AINSLEY. Well, we're going to have to move

along. I appreciate your calling, but if you can't narrow in on the problem, we can hardly give you an answer.

BORIS. Ahh. Beautiful day!

JACOB. Do you want to play a little canasta?

BORIS. No, I don't like canasta. How about bridge? Anyone want to play bridge?

JACOB. It's a boring game.

BORIS. And canasta isn't?

JACOB. Canasta's got a little life . . . a little spunk.

ESTHER. What's wrong with bridge?

JACOB. I told you. It's dull.

ESTHER. I've got a headache.

JACOB. If only the humidity would let up.

BORIS. What do you mean? There's no humidity. It's a perfectly clear day.

ESTHER. You don't have any trouble with your sinuses?

BORIS. No. My sinuses are perfect. I just went to the doctor. He said I have the heart and lungs of a twenty-five-year-old man.

ESTHER. So how long do you think you're going to live?

JACOB. Everything else is falling apart.

BORIS. If I die tomorrow, I'll still have better lungs than you do.

6

I was a brilliant scholar, well versed in the subtleties of the Gemara and the complexities of the Kabbalah. Yet I remained a troubled man, bewildered about the course and purpose of my life. One evening, while contemplating suicide, I overheard two students speak fervently of the Zaddik of Rome. Perhaps this famous wise man possessed the answers I needed. I decided to go and see for myself if the master's teachings justified his reputation. I put on my hat, my coat, packed an overnight bag, and traveled on foot to Rome. When I reached the Zaddik's house and finally stood before him, I waited for the Zaddik to speak profoundly. But the Zaddik only told me that once a surgeon was called to a great house where an operation was performed on him. After this, he dismissed me.

I took a room for the night at a local inn.

The following evening I again went to the Zaddik's house. Surely tonight I would hear something of the master's wisdom. But all the Zaddik told me was that once a famous prosecutor found himself guilty as charged.

I did not know what to make of these parables.

When I returned to the inn, I collected my belongings, paid the bill, and hired a driver for the journey home. We would start as soon as the weather cleared. But around midnight, as the full moon appeared, a man from the Zaddik burst in with a message. I was to visit the Zaddik immediately. I left at once. This time the Zaddik received me in his study. He told me that a great engineer awoke one evening in just such a room, and that upon rising and gazing into a mirror, he found himself transformed into a holy man. An official dispatch slipped under his door brought him back to his senses. The letter requested his immediate departure for headquarters. He caught the next train that passed through his provincial town only to find himself trapped in a car crowded with refugees. He miraculously eluded death and escaped by cutting his way through barbed wire.

Then he traveled north until he reached the retreat of the Messiah, who was planting trees in the moonlight.

Bewildered by this absurd and extraordinary story, I interrupted the Zaddik. "Why are you telling me this?" Staring fiercely at me, the Zaddik removed his outer garment, revealing an S.S. uniform, and announced himself as Captain Kreitz of the Secret Police. He scornfully placed me under arrest. Two soldiers entered and took me to a van parked at the curb. But on the way to the prison, the van was forced off the road, I was rescued by the underground, and I was taken to the real Zaddik of Rome, who, disguised as a Nazi officer, was vacationing in Palermo.

When we reached the Zaddik's house and I finally stood before the master—resplendent in a black uniform with a death's head, cross-bones, and an Iron Cross—I waited for the Zaddik to utter his teachings so that I might weigh them. But the Zaddik only told me that once a surgeon was called to a great house where an operation was performed on him. After this, he dismissed me.

I took a room at a local inn. All night long I labored at the blueprints for the chambers on my drawing board.

The next evening I again went to the Zaddik's house. But all the Zaddik told me was that once a famous prosecutor found himself guilty as charged.

I did not know what to make of these parables.

When I returned to the inn, I collected my belongings, paid the bill, and caught the next train for Berlin.

MESSIAH. *Little by little, time kills all our illusions. Pipes rust . . . paints peel off . . . arteries harden . . . brains soften . . . gums bleed . . . teeth rot . . . lovers leave . . . friends flee . . .*

What has become of us? We are no longer firm bright apples on the firm bright tree of life. We are a mess of rotting applesauce. A change has come over the world. Dark thoughts are born. Dark deeds ripen in the midst of their vapors. The eye of God no longer shines on us. Where once it shone there is nothing now but an empty, burned-out socket.

I'll buy a gas station or open a small TV repair shop in Tampa. I'll marry an attractive divorcee—a clerk who sells beauty products in a department store. She'll be tired of sleeping with people in motels that are so well lit outside you can never get the room dark enough. She'll marry me because she'll want a stable home life. We'll sit in the backyard of our trailer on those chairs with straps on them, next to a chipped birdbath. We'll grow old together. Then, one day, I'll get a hernia when I'm fishing in my small boat and hook a cinderblock. I'll develop prostate trouble and get cancer of the nose. She'll become religious. She'll turn to Jesus—who has snake hips, is quite lean, blond, a pretty fair surfer, has a beautiful tenor voice, plays the pedal steel guitar, and would be a very fine dirt-bike scrambler except for his robes.

She'll go to church wearing a shiny blue suit with frills around the neck, a hat with a little bunch of cherries, a purse, gloves, and sensible shoes.

And there will be no scroll in our doorway . . . only the totemic pink flamingo, made of plaster of Paris, on our front lawn.

7

Cleaned out Hoffman's apartment. Gave most of his belongings to local charities. Kept a prayer shawl, some books of mysticism and poetry, a ram's horn, and a Bible. Also uncovered, in the back of his closet, a neatly folded black uniform, a riding crop, boots, and a cap with the insignia of a lightning bolt.

Hoffman's journal closed with a description of Dreamland, the amusement park in Orlando. The work going on at the space center there, he wrote, was extremely promising. In fact, he'd booked himself on the inaugural flight of its rocket ship, rumored to be capable of unprecedented speed. I found the ticket in the back of the journal. I decided to drive up and see for myself.

In Dreamland. Strolling along the midway. I pass rides . . . exhibits . . . concessions. Then I see the spaceship poised on its platform. A crowd is gathered around it, listening to the speech of a tour guide.

TOUR GUIDE. What first attracted explorers to Florida was the legend of a Fountain of Youth. Soon, entrepreneurs and fortune hunters, as well as the old, sick, and dying, came here in search of the restorative spring. The Fountain was never discovered. But in its place a rocketship has been built that can transcend the speed of light and reverse the aging process. Tickets are available in both first class and coach. . . .

I give Hoffman's ticket to the guard at the gate, walk up the ramp, and enter.

STEWARDESS. Flight 66 is now ready for departure. Please check that your seat belt is securely fastened and your seat upright for lift-off.

MISSION CONTROL. Launch sequence. Five . . . four . . . three . . . two . . . one . . . ignition.

BLAST OFF

We've crash-landed in a swamp. The ship is a smoking ruin. We spend most of our time jumping from behind rocks, springing out of trees, emerging from holes in the ground, and dragging ancient and useless electrical household appliances behind us.

Yes, hundreds of years have passed into the future. We've learned there was a war, concussions from nuclear explosions altering the earth's axis, causing the polar icecaps to melt, flooding coastal areas so that New York, from which so many members of our group originally migrated to Florida, was buried three hundred feet under the ocean, fishes swimming in and out of the windows of the city.

And now the members of our expedition serve as Wise Men and Women. We write histories, books on ancient technology, and go on long hikes in the mountains, through fields of flaming Alpine flour, a cup of vinegar, some thorns, and a pair of sandals, and I dreamt I woke up dreaming again, or was I still awake dreaming I was asleep under a fountain with a tank of ice water, a spout, and a dispenser with paper cups, thinking: Listen, just bring me a mint, coffee, and a pillow, and I'll try to relax. Do you have any Dramamine? I think I'm out of my depth. You see, my problem is whenever I go to a funeral I don't know whether to laugh, cry, or demonstrate floral arrangements. I've failed to adopt a point of view over Palestine—or Miami, for that matter—is glorious. The shrines, the fossils, the history, the sheer incoherence of it all is a form of amnesia, like being trapped in a burning temple wearing a pair of shorts and suspenders and performing in a traditional folk dance, thinking: Help *me* . . . save *me* . . . catalog *me* . . . look *me* up in books to find out who *I* am . . . what *I've* done . . . and I'll say, "Thank you. Thank you very much. Very nice of you. I appreciate it. I really do. You have a kind heart. A good soul. I won't forget this. Ever again."